NO ESCAPE!

He was driving them in evasive maneuvers now, while the hull crashed like a gong, and flashes of enemy force were plain in the simultaneous overload of instruments. Flash and crash again, blinding stroke from the enemy and blending sigh of their own weapons lashing back, more in defiance than in any true hope of damaging Goliath. The berserker which had caught them by surprise was too big to fight, too fast to get away from, here in relatively open space. Nothing to do but dodge—

Yet again the berserker struck . . .

Tor books by Fred Saberhagen

THE BERSERKER SERIES
The Berserker Wars
Berserker Base (with Poul Anderson, Ed Bryant, Stephen Donaldson, Larry Niven, Connie Willis, and Roger Zelazny)
Berserker: Blue Death
The Berserker Throne
Berkerker's Planet

THE DRACULA SERIES
The Dracula Tapes
The Holmes-Dracula Files
An Old Friend of the Family
Thorn
Dominion
A Matter of Taste

THE SWORDS SERIES
The First Book of Swords
The Second Book of Swords
The Third Book of Swords
The First Book of Lost Swords: Woundhealer's Story
The Second Book of Lost Swords: Sightblinder's Story
The Third Book of Lost Swords: Stonecutter's Story
The Fourth Book of Lost Swords: Farslayer's Story
The Fifth Book of Lost Swords: Coinspinner's Story
The Sixth Book of Lost Swords: Mindsword's Story

OTHER BOOKS
A Century of Progress
Coils (with Roger Zelazny)
Earth Descended
The Mask of the Sun
A Question of Time
Specimens
The Veils of Azlaroc
The Water of Thought

FRED SABERHAGEN

BERSERKER MAN

A TOM DOHERTY ASSOCIATES BOOK
NEW YORK

This is a work of fiction. All the characters and events portrayed in this book are fictitious, and any resemblance to real people or events is purely coincidental.

BERSERKER MAN

A Tor Book
Published by Tom Doherty Associates, Inc.
49 West 24th Street
New York, N.Y. 10010

TOR® is a registered trademark of Tom Doherty Associates, Inc.

Cover art by Tony Roberts

ISBN:0-812-50564-6

First Tor printing: April 1992

Printed in the United States of America

0 9 8 7 6 5 4 3 2 1

PROLOGUE

WELL, ELLY TEMESVAR THOUGHT GRAYLY, WE'VE GIVEN it a good fight, done better than anyone might have expected, considering how little ship we have to fight it with.

Out perpendicularly from the surface of a peculiar star there jutted what looked like a transfixing spear of plasma, bright as the star itself, as thick as a major planet, and so long that it looked needle-thin. On the jet's brilliant, almost insubstantial surface the little duoship that Elly and her partner rode in clung like a microbe on a glowing treetrunk, in an effort to find concealment where there was really none. And somewhere on the other side of the shining plasma fountain, a hundred thousand kilometers or more away, the mad berserker stalked them. Berserkers were pure machine, of course, but still in Elly's most heartsure mental images of them they were all mad—she smelled on them the suicidal madness of their ancient and unknown builders.

The odd star that drained itself into the plasma jet was close enough to have been blinding were not the ports all sealed opaque for combat. And despite the nearness of the Galactic Core, few other stars were visible. Bright nebular material filled cubic parsec after cubic parsec in this region, hiding everything else and evoking old legends of lightspace in which the stars were only points of darkness.

"Pull in the scanning nodes just a touch on your side, Elly." Frank's voice, as usual sounding almost imperturbable, came into her earphones. He was on the other side of the thick steel bulkhead that completely bisected crew quarters when its hatches were closed for combat. In theory one compartment might be breached, while the human in the other one survived to fight on. In practice, this time, the whole craft was just about to be crunched like a pretzel, and Elly in moments of free mental time wished that she might have, at the end, at least as much human contact as open connecting hatches could provide.

She did not voice her wish. "Nodes in," she acknowledged instead, in trained reaction that seemed to function independent of her will. Her fingers had meanwhile remained poised but motionless upon the ten keys of her auxiliary controls. Through her helmet the electrical waves of her brain directly drove the equipment for which she was responsible, in a control system that worked a large fraction of a second faster than any dependent upon arm-length nerves.

"It's going to come again—" The rest of Frank's warning was lost, even with earphones, as the berserker came, wolf springing from behind a plasma tree. Basic control of the ship depended upon the signals from her partner's brain, and the stroke and counterstroke of the next passage at arms were over before Elly had fully grasped that it was about to start. One reason Frank Marcus sat as commander in the left seat was that he was faster than Elly by far; but then he was faster than anyone. Frank the Legendary. Even two minutes ago, Elly had still nursed conscious hopes that he might be able to get them out of this alive.

He was driving them in evasive maneuvers now, while the hull crashed like a gong, and flashes of enemy force were plain in the simultaneous overload of instruments. Flash and crash again, blinding stroke from the enemy and blending sigh of their own weapons lashing back, more in defiance than in any true hope of damaging Goliath. The berserker which had caught them by surprise was too big to fight, too fast to get away from, here in relatively open space. Nothing to do but dodge—

Yet again the berserker struck, and yet again they emerged whole from the barrage. They were characters in some fantasy cartoon, staggering along a tightrope and parrying a rain of meteoric irons with the flimsy stalk of a broken umbrella.

"—little ship—"

Between great blasts of static, that was the voice of the berserker reaching them. It was trying to talk, only to distract them perhaps, or perhaps to offer life of a sort. There were sometimes living, willing servitors. And sometimes there were specimens that the unliving enemy found interesting enough to be kept breathing for a long time under study. Distraction, with the game effectively over, might seem a pointless waste of tactical finesse, but the enemy's tactics were varied by randomizing devices and tended to be unpredictable.

"—tle ship, new weapons will not save you—"

The voice was quavering, neither male nor female, neither old nor young. It was assembled from the recorded words of prisoners, of goodlife (the willing servitors), of defiant human enemies who had cursed the thing before they died and whose very curses were put to its use.

"New weapons? What the hell does that mean?" Like many who fought berserkers, Frank Marcus seemed to believe in Hell, at least enough to swear by it.

"That's what it said."

"—helpless ... badlife ..." A great static roar. "You are too small ..." The message or distraction from the enemy dissolved utterly in noise. No carrier wave could any longer bring it through the furious radiation from the plasma jet.

Mumbling something to himself, Frank danced the duoship around the jet. He dropped his craft from normal space into that condition called flight-space, where physical existence outside the guarded hull became little more than mathematics, and out-racing light became not only possible but unavoidable. He brought them bursting back again into normal space, a fearful risk this near the great mass of a star. He had a way, had luck, had something no one could bottle or even measure, that in addition to his speed made for success against berserkers. Elly had heard the claim that, given a thousand human pilots with this potency, humanity might have won the long war centuries ago. Cloning of his cells had been tried, to produce a race of Franks, but the results had been disappointing.

Just behind them—so Elly read the flickerings that raced across her panels—the jet-star's solar wind exploded like the surface of a wavy pond attacked by a sharp-skipping pebble. A chain of blasts expanded into spheres of force and gas. Behind them too, delayed but not avoided, the pursuing monster came, its prey once more in view. The berserker made a dark, irregular blot against giant swirls of bright nebula that were far too distant to provide a hiding place, the stuff of the galaxy in an agelong expulsion from the galactic heart. The enemy was a tiny blot a hundred kilometers across.

Frank would never quit. In a hundred and forty milliseconds he skipped his ship through a distance equal to the diameter of Earth's orbit, whipping it once more out of normal space and once more back, intact, a blind man safely juggling razors.

This time, space around them was different when they came back. White noise on Elly's viewscreen. Peculiar readings everywhere—but at the same time silence, and stability.

"Frank?"

"Yeah. We're inside the jet, Elly. As I figured, it turned out to be a hollow tube. We're riding it out away from the star at a couple hundred kilometers per second. The boogie's still outside."

"You . . . it . . . how can you tell?"

Something resembling amusement shaded Frank's business voice. "If it was in here with us, it'd still be trying to chew us up, right?"

"Oh." She hadn't heard such meekness in her own shipboard voice for years. That word had come out in a novice trainee's timid chirp; she had heard the like from a good many of them during her tour as instructor at Space Combat School.

Frank was talking. "So, it's going to know we're here in the tube—because there's nowhere else we can be. It'll try to get a fix on just where we are inside—probably won't be able to. Then it'll come in after us. It'll come fairly slowly. It must compute it has us cold, and it has no reason to take the kind of chance we just did. As soon as it does come in, we go."

"Where?"

"Yeah, that's the question." Again in Frank's voice a shade of humor, this time laced with bitterness. Then, a new note of urgent thought: "Elly.

Take a look at that cloud down at the end of this pipe. Ever see anything like that before?"

She adjusted her instruments, and learned to begin with that the inner surface of the great jet bearing them along was about five thousand kilometers away, as they rode near its center. Directly behind them was the sun that fueled and projected the enormous jet, and hurled down its hollow center a torrent of particle radiation from which the duoship's hull had so far shielded its occupants. While directly ahead . . .

There their strange jet fed a nebula perhaps even stranger, one which at their present speed they should reach in less than an hour. Elly scanned it as best she could, and made very little sense of what her instruments reported. The nebula seemed to be emitting fiercely at many wavelengths while absorbing greedily at others . . . for a moment she thought there was a grand pattern to be detected, but the indications for order were fleeting and in another moment chaos had intervened. Go into that in flightspace? she thought. It's far too dense. We'll hit it like a solid wall . . .

"Hey, Elly?" The voice in her earphones was suddenly much changed, with a difference she did not at first comprehend.

She answered numbly: "What?"

"Come over, will you? We've got a solid quarter hour before there's anything we need to do."

She might have said that there was nothing they could do, now or in fifteen minutes. But she unfastened herself from the clasp of her acceleration couch and drifted free of it, a blonde young woman, large and strong. The artificial gravity was now set in combat mode, operating only as needed to counter otherwise unbearable accelerations.

As Elly moved to open one of the hatches communicating with the other half of the ship's living space, some thoughts about a last goodbye were skipping through her mind. And something about suicide, which she would prefer to being captured live by a berserker.

Most of the space in the commander's small cabin was occupied by Frank's acceleration couch and by his body. It was not easy to see just where the one ended and the other began. Photographs Elly had seen of Frank, made before that brush with a berserker nine years back had almost cost him his life, showed a trim-waisted, young-looking man, so intense that even his image seemed to thrum with extra energy. Now, what the berserker and the surgeons had left of that vital body was permanently cushioned in fluids and encased in armor.

The three cable-connected units in which Frank lived struck Elly sometimes as a lazy costumer's concept of an insect body. There were head, thorax, and abdomen, but no face to turn to Elly as she entered. She knew, though, that Frank would be watching her with a part of his instrument-perceptions, while he remained wired directly to the sensors of the ship, and adequately alert. One plastic-and-metal arm rose from the central box to acknowledge her presence with a small wave.

Elly's eyes and ears and mind still rang with battle; she felt half-stunned into stupidity. "What?" she asked again, into the silence.

"Just wanted to enjoy your company." Frank's voice, sounding completely human and natural, issued now from a speaker near her head. The arm, too thin and too lacking in fingers to be human, meanwhile extended itself a little farther and stroked her shoulder. Its hand slid along to her waist. The familiar feel of it was not unpleasant; its movement was gentle and its texture smooth, like warm skin. Something about it, maybe the hardness of the underlying structure, always gave

Elly the sensation of encountering powerful masculinity.

Now the arm began to tug her drifting figure toward the body-boxes on their segmented couch, and now she understood at last. "You're crazy!" The words broke from her almost in a laugh, but still with something like conviction.

"Why crazy? I told you, we've got fifteen minutes." Frank wouldn't be, couldn't be, wrong about a thing like that. When Frank went off duty, it was safe to go. "Sorry if you're not in the mood. Imagine a great big kiss, right about here." His voice performed a cheerful sound-effect. Another hand, this one partly of flesh (and feeling no more and no less strong and sure and male because of that) came from somewhere and went to work with an infinitely sure touch upon the clasps of the single garment that Elly routinely wore inside her couch.

She closed her eyes, despaired of being able to think of anything important like suicide and good-bye, and ceased to try. The inner surfaces of the artifact-abdomen, evolving to embrace her as she let herself be drawn against them, were not cold or metallic. As usual at this point, she had a moment of feeling rather ridiculous, being reminded of a leathery vaulting horse that she had straddled in some gym class long ago. And now, once more, the touch of human flesh . . .

Frank had said fifteen minutes. In less than twelve, Elly was safely and snugly back in her own combat couch, tuned in on all her instruments and ready for business. Trust Commander Frank to see to it that nothing interfered with that. All hatches were once more closed solidly again, as per regulations. Combat was now imminent, whereas twelve minutes back it had not been.

Years ago Elly had realized that Elly Temesvar,

shunned by some men as too overpowering in several ways, couldn't begin to sustain any close personal relationship with this sometime shipmate of hers. She never felt so much used, abused, liked, disliked, or loved by him as she felt simply befuddled. *Her* thoughts and feelings about *him* ... it was as if she never was given a change to develop any. Perhaps any she did start to develop, good or bad, were blown and swept away as soon as they began to sprout, by some contrary aspect of the man. He simply did too much and knew too much and was too much. Off duty she tended to avoid Frank Marcus, and tended not to talk about him, even when the curious pressed for information.

Thirteen minutes of the fifteen gone, and now Frank began to explain his developing plan, if that was the right word, for their next tactic. If it was suicidal, she thought, at least it was grander and dicier than swallowing any little pills.

Meanwhile the odd nebula at the approaching end of the great glowing tunnel continued to fly closer. And now the last of Frank's quarter-hour passed, marked by no event more vital than an increasing flickering and tattering of the tunnel's plasma wall, which here began to churn almost like a mass of falling water. The jet was now starting to disperse, the speed of its material increasing rapidly, evidently because distance was freeing it from the enormous gravity of the star from which it issued.

"Here we go," her earphones said. "It's coming any moment."

The small ship bounced with the turbulence of the unraveling of the distant plasma walls that had for a little while concealed it. Elly manned her post, though what she could do for the ship just now was trivial. Through a tattering wall of the stuff that hurtled outward from the star, the great berserker came.

ONE

THE CARVING, ACCORDING TO ITS LABEL, WAS OF *LESHY*
wood, described as native to the planet Alpine and
difficult to work as well as enduring and beautiful. Angelo Lombok, a stranger to this stuff and to
this world as well, turned it over in his fingers,
pondering. It was certified as an original hand-
work, and the artist did not appear to have been
bothered by the reputed difficulty. The basic style
was the same as that of the Geulincx carvings
Lombok had been shown before leaving Earth, but
the subject matter was more disturbing. It showed
a man and a woman, fugitives, for their bodies
leaned forward on long-striding legs even as their
anxious faces turned to look behind them. The
swirls of wooden clothing were somewhat over-
dramatic, but what could you expect from an artist ten years old?

Sometimes Lombok wished that he had in one
way or another gone in more seriously for art.

Well, one only had a single lifetime to spend, four or five hundred years at the outside; and he had now invested too much of his in work along another line to consider starting over.

With a faint sigh, he stretched up on his toes to set the carving back upon the giftshop shelf— which, no doubt, silently recorded the replacement, and forebore to sound an alarm when he turned away. The one bag he had brought with him was small and light, and he needed no help to carry it through the modest bustle of the passenger terminal and outside to where a string of compact aircraft waited to be hired.

Looking something like a tiny brown woodcarving himself, Lombok settled into a comfortable seat aboard the next conveyance to glide up to the dock, and issued orders.

"I wish to visit the family Geulincx." It came out *Jew-links*, which he had been informed was the locally correct pronunciation. He suspected that, like many other famous and semi-famous people, the Geulincx clan had programmed obstacles into their local transport control system to forestall unknown visitors; and these obstacles he now endeavored to bypass. "I am not expected, but they will want to see me; I represent the Academy, on Earth, and I am here to offer their son Michel a scholarship."

He had the co-ordinates of the place ready to supply if necessary, but the machine evidently did not need them. It seemed his ploy had worked, for in a moment he was on his way, the rim of the spaceport dropping away smoothly beneath the climbing vehicle and a forested mountain leaning closer. Some of the flora here, he had been informed, was Earth-descended, as were of course the colonists. Upon a crag that slid past now he recognized bristlecone pines, close-molded to the rock by centuries of wind.

His flight among the mountains, here only thinly inhabited, took him into the advancing night. As soon as the cloudless sky began to darken there appeared overhead part of the planet's network of defensive satellites, celestial clockwork in a slowly shifting pattern. There were no real stars, but also to be seen in the jeweled velvet of this almost-private space were the faint, untwinkling sparks of three natural planets and two small moons, all now surrounded and enfolded by what looked like an infinity of never-ending night. That engulfing blackness was all dark nebula, called Blackwool by the natives. It was thick enough to blot out, even here, the Core itself, and the realization of that fact made Lombok uncomfortable—whereas, of course, he would have been unaffected by the familiar and infinitely vaster looming of the stars.

The military situation in the Alpine system had not yet deteriorated to the point where blackouts were in order, and the Geulincx chalet, halfway up another mountainside, was almost gaily lighted. It was a consciously pretty building, in a half-timbered style evidently copied from something in Earth's long past—he had seen its picture used in the family advertisements in the art journals. When he was sure that he had almost reached his goal, Lombok opened his small valise and riffled once more through the papers carried on top. All in order. All perfectly convincing, or had better be.

A road, devoid of traffic save for what appeared to be one heavy hauler, whose headlights revealed the narrow pavement, came winding upward from the valley floor. Other dwellings must be even rarer here than near the spaceport, if one could judge by the lack of other lights. The landing deck at the chalet, though, was well illuminated, with one empty aircraft parked and waiting at one side of it. Lombok landed gently under soft floodlights, just as a man and a woman, no doubt alerted by some detection system, came out of the main building a few meters away to stand and watch. His cashcard in a slot conferred payment on the machine. A moment later Lombok was standing on the deck, valise in hand, while his transportation whirred away behind him.

The man, tall and gray, watched it go as if he might have liked to keep it waiting for a visitor, or impostor, whose stay would probably be brief. The woman came forward, though, hand outstretched and ready to be eager. "Mr. Lombok? Did I hear your recording in the flyer correctly, something about the Academy, and a scholarship—?"

"I trust you did." Her hand enveloped his; she was broadly built and muscular, and Lombok's briefing on earth had informed him that she had been a successful athlete in her first youth.

"I'm Carmen Geulincx, of course, and this is Sixtus. Let us take that bag for you." Lombok's briefing had informed him also that on Alpine a woman generally took her husband's family name. Sixtus, taller, grayer, older than his wife, now came forward, cordial in a quiet way now that it seemed that there was nothing else for him to be. For a few moments they all stood there in the fine evening—it occurred to the visitor that daytime in the lower altitudes must be quite hot—exchanging pleasantries, about Lombok's journey as if he were an invited guest, and about the beauty of the spot, which he was sure he would appreciate come dawn.

"And now—what is this, Mr. Lombok, about a scholarship?"

He twinkled at them reassuringly, and put a small hand through each of their arms. "Perhaps we should go in, where you can sit down and brace yourselves for a pleasant shock. We would like Michel—how is he, by the way?"

"Oh, fine," the woman murmured impatiently, with a quick glance toward the house. "What—?"

"We would like to pay his way—and that of at least one adult parent or guardian—to come to Earth and study with us at the Academy. For four years."

The woman literally swayed.

Five minutes later they were in the house, but no one had really sat down as yet. Carmen was moving this way and that in excitement, piling up false starts toward sitting beside her guest (who kept jumping up from the sofa out of politeness, and being urged to sit again) and organizing some kind of meal or snack by way of beginning a celebration.

Meanwhile Sixtus stood leaning in a timbered doorway, with the look of a man thinking and thinking. He had, very early in the discussion, hinted that he would like to see Lombok's credentials, which had been immediately produced, and were impeccable.

"The thing is . . . " murmured Lombok, as soon as a sort of temporary calm had established itself.

Sixtus shot a glance that said: *I knew there was a catch*. His wife did not receive it, being suddenly fixated, with a stricken look, upon her visitor.

"What?" she breathed.

"The thing is, that there is very little time in which this particular opening can be filled. You understand some of our most generous grants and bequests impose conditions upon us that we do not like, but still must honor. This opening, as I say, must be filled quickly. It will be necessary for Michel to come at once. Within two days he must start for Earth."

"But there's no *ship* . . . is there?"

"Fortunately, the convoy I arrived with is laying over for a day or two. The decision to offer Michel the scholarship was reached only about six months ago, on Earth, and I was immediately dispatched. Luckily there was a convoy scheduled. There was no time to send you any preliminary announcement, or ask if you would accept."

"Oh, we quite understand *that*. And naturally anyone involved in Art"—the capitalization was audible—"would just . . . of course there's no real hesitance about accepting. But only two days?"

"That is when the convoy leaves. And who knows when the next ship will be available? Earth as you know is months away."

"Oh, we know." Somewhere in the reaches of the house below, a muted rumble: logs, perhaps, being dumped from that heavy hauler.

"I understand that this is very short notice to give you. But at the same time it is a very rare opportunity. All of us at the Academy have been much impressed by the examples of Michel's work that have reached us."

"The agent said his stuff was beginning to sell on Earth. But I never . . . oh. Only two days. Sixtus, what—?"

Sixtus nodded, smiled, shook his head a little in various directions. Below, more noise, a power saw ripping with good appetite at wood, no doubt producing a texture more modern cutting devices could not duplicate. There were, Lombok had been told, a small army of workers here: cabinet makers, carvers, apprentices.

He remarked into the tense silence, "I noticed one of Michel's carvings on sale at the spaceport gift shop. I've really been looking forward to meeting him. Is he—?"

"Oh, of *course*. He'll be very anxious to meet you. I think he's probably working now." Carmen cast vague, anxious eyes upward.

They led Lombok up some stairs, then along a hall. Sixtus, who had acquired Lombak's bag, dropped it en passant into the open doorway of a dim, pine-scented bedroom. The house's interior was as luxurious and calculatedly rustic as its outside.

Of several rugged doors near the end of the hallway, one was ajar. Carmen pushed it gently open, peering in ahead of the two men. "Michel? We have a surprise guest, and he'd like to see you."

The room was large, even for a bedchamber-workshop combined, and as well lighted as a jeweler's showplace. There was a rumpled bed at the far end, piled with oversized pillows, against a row of windows now darkened by the night outside. Their draperies hung open as if forgotten.

Against the wall beside the door, a long elaborate workbench stood piled with woodworking equipment and stocks of material. Midway along the bench, the boy perched on a stool. A ten-year-old with long, faded hair, he looked back at Lombok solemnly as the small man entered.

"Hello, Michel."

"Hello." The boy's voice was thin and ordinary. His coloring was not blond so much as dusty-colorless. A narrow face and large, washed-out looking eyes made him appear frail, but he took Lombok's hand firmly enough and looked him boldly in the eye. He was barefoot and wearing what looked like pajamas, ingrained with wood dust and fine shavings, as if he had spent the day in them.

"Oh, Michel," Carmen said, "why didn't you

change? Mr. Lombok will think you're ill, too ill for a . . . how would you like to go on a long trip, Sweetie?"

Michel slid off his stool and stood scratching the back of one knee with the opposite foot. "Where?"

"Earth," said Lombok, speaking as to an adult. "I'm authorized to offer you a scholarship to the Academy."

Michel's eyebrows went up just a notch—and then his face was normalized by a very natural ten-year-old smile.

Ten minutes after that, the adults had adjourned to a terrace, where a gentle aura of infrared from some concealed source kept off what must be the night's increasing chill, and warm drinks were brought by an efficient robot rolling on almost silent wheels.

"You must be very proud of him," Lombok remarked, taking his first sip, watching the others carefully.

"Couldn't be more if we were his bioparents," Sixtus put in. "We're both of us carvers, too, of course—they certainly did a superb job of genetic matching at the adoption center."

Lombok sipped his drink once more, carefully, and put it down. "I didn't realize he was adopted," he lied, in tones of mild interest.

"Oh yes. He knows, of course."

"It occurs to me—may I ask a somewhat personal question?"

"Please do."

"Well. I was wondering if you had ever made any effort to find out who his bioparents were, or are?"

His hosts both shook their heads, amused. Sixtus assured him, "The Premier of Alpine himself couldn't get information out of that place. They keep the medical profiles of the bioparents available, for health reasons. But that's all they ever give out—nothing else, once the bioparents say they want it sealed."

"I see." Lombok pondered. "Even so, I think I shall have to try, tomorrow. The assistant director has a pet project, you see, correlating bioparents' behavior and lifestyle with the children's artistic achievement. Is this adoption center on Alpine?"

"In Glacier City. But I'm sure going there won't do you any good."

"I suppose not, but I'll have to report that I made the effort. In the morning, I'll fly over there. And then—am I to take it that our offer is accepted?"

Before he got an answer, Michel himself, now fully if casually dressed, came with quick eagerness out onto the terrace and dropped into a chair. "My, such energy," his mother teased.

The boy was looking keenly at the visitor. "Have you ever seen a berserker?" he demanded directly, evidently following some train of his own thoughts with youthful single-mindedness.

Sixtus chuckled, and Lombok tried to make a little joke of it. "No, I'm still healthy." That of course was no answer at all, and he saw that Michel expected one. "No, I haven't. I've never been on a planet under direct attack. I don't travel in space a great deal. My trip out here was, as I mentioned, uneventful in the way of military action. Thanks to a strong convoy, and/or good fortune."

"No alarms at the Bottleneck?" This from Sixtus. "You must have come through that way." A painful truism, for there was no other way to reach the Alpine system, surrounded as it was by parsec after parsec of dust and gas, too thick for any practical astrogation.

"No trouble," Lombok reiterated. He studied the adults' faces. "I know, some folks would feel alarmed at the prospect of a long space voyage just now. But let's face it, the way things are going, Alpine itself is not going to be the safest spot in the inhabited galaxy. If and when the Bottleneck does close completely, either as a result of nebular drift or through berserker action—well, everyone on Alpine is going to be in a state of siege at best."

He was not telling the Geulincx clan anything they did not already know. But he was discussing the very chancy essentials of their future, and all three were watching him and listening with the utmost concentration. He went on: "Speaking for myself, I feel more comfortable making the trip back now than I would staying."

Sixtus was looking up at the nebular night, like some farmer judging when a wild thunderstorm was likely to assault his tender crops. "I have to stay here for the sake of the business," he announced. "There are other members of the family depending on it. I have a sister—she has children. And there are workers, dealers—I can't just pack up and leave on two days' notice."

"The business is important," Carmen agreed. She and her husband were looking at each other as if they had independently arrived at the whole solution, to the surprise of neither. "But then, Michel's future is, also." Her marveling lips formed the next words in silence: *The Academy*!

"The convoy leaves in two days," Lombok prodded. "Two days at the outside. They've promised me a few hours' notice." In fact the fleet would move when he told the admiral he was ready; but no one on Alpine, Lombok hoped, dreamed as much.

"He must go," said Carmen, and stroked her

son's long hair. His eyes were shining with anticipation. "And he's simply too young to go alone.
Sixtus, how long do you think it will take you to
get things in order here, and join us?"

Lombok drew on the smoker he had just lighted,
meanwhile watching the others reflectively. The
lady was more excited than her son; she must see
an old dream come to life, herself at the Academy
where she would move among the famous people
of the world of high-priced art; with her energy
and cleverness and her son's talent that world
would lie open before them. . . . The man at Moonbase who had sent Lombok had calculated well.

Lombok in his mind's eye saw her at Moonbase,
stunned, perhaps outraged when she learned the
truth. The truth-telling would have to be handled
carefully, when the time came.

TWO

THE EDUCATIONAL SYSTEM ON ALPINE WAS QUITE FLEX-
ible, and he hadn't spent much time in formal
schooling. Also the isolation of the family establishment had tended to diminish contacts with
other children. The result was that he had only a
few friends near his own age, a lack that had never
notably concerned him.

Of those few, he could think of none that he was
really going to miss. But when, in the morning,
after Mr. Lombok had departed on what everyone
had agreed must be a futile mission to the adoption center, Michel's mother suggested that he call
one or two of the children at least to say goodbye,
he complied. Of the three he called, two were
bored by his great news—or tried to sound that
way. The third, awed and openly envious, wondered aloud how Michel felt about going through
the Bottleneck, where there was almost certain to
be fighting.

Michel, who was somewhat keen on space war—at least as it was fought in the juvenile adventure books—and considered himself a well-informed layperson on the subject, estimated the risks as somewhat lower. After all, the ship captains and the other folk in charge would not decide to risk the passage if they thought it prohibitively dangerous.

Mr. Lombok was back in a couple of hours, announcing that he had been unable to learn anything, but not looking disappointed. Were Carmen and Michel ready? He was going to call the spaceport, on the chance that it had been decided to move up departure time and they had not got around to notifying him . . .

"Good thing I did," he announced, a couple of minutes later, turning away from the privacy of the communicator console. "Good thing you're ready, too! The last shuttle lifts off three hours from now."

It took the four of them something over an hour in a family aircraft to reach the port. Michel had visited it twice before, once on a tour with his school class, and again to see off a visiting uncle from Esteel. This time he said goodbye to his father on the ramp, feeling a moment of sharp sadness as they embraced. Then the three travelers were hurried into a shuttle, a larger craft than that which had borne away the uncle, and with its hull bearing a hash of letters and numbers, some military designation.

His first shuttle flight did not feel all that different from a straight climb in an aircraft, at first. He and his mother and Mr. Lombok were the only passengers; as the sky outside the cleared ports purpled and darkened, a young woman wearing the insignia of an ensign in the personnel services came to sit with them and chat. No one but Michel seemed to notice when the artificial gravity came on in the cabin. He did, though, subtle as the difference was; and felt immediately afterward how the great thrustors underneath began to multiply their force.

And as the blue of atmospheric daylight faded, he began to be able to see some of the convoy escorting them; Mr. Lombok had spoken reassuringly but vaguely of its strength. There were six good-sized ships hanging in formation, small crescent sun-glints against the starless black. But wait—there rode six more, in another flight higher up. And wait again, six more beyond . . .

When he had counted six flights of warships waiting, and understood that there might be more beyond his range of vision, he began to wonder what was going on. More avidly than his parents realized, he followed the news of the war in space, and not all the books he read on the subject were juvenile novels. A collection of ships this strong ought to be called a task force or a battle fleet. Mr. Lombok had implied that this force had come more or less straight out to Alpine from Earth, and that it was now going straight back. For what?

His mother dutifully noted the various flights of warships as he pointed them out to her, smiled at his keenness, and went on rehearsing for Mr. Lombok the speeches she meant to use on important people when they got to the Academy. Mr. Lombok, now looking totally relaxed, gave her his smiling attention, only now and then directing a sort of proprietary glance toward Michel.

Only when the starship in which they were to ride at last loomed overhead, like a continent of metal dimly lighted from below by Alpine's blue-glowing dayside, did Carmen at last take a real look.

"I'll certainly feel safe on that," she commented, peering upward, and then looked round to make sure that their meager baggage had not somehow crept away and lost itself.

Michel observed the docking as best he could; and before the shuttle was swallowed inside the block-thick hull of the leviathan, he had the chance to glimpse her name, running in comparatively modest letters across her skin of battle gray: she was the *Johann Karlsen*.

He sat there looking out the port at nearly featureless dark metal, about a meter from his nose. Then the convoy, or fleet, was not only sizable, but contained at least one vessel of the dreadnought class: the very one aboard which he and his mother were about to have the fun of a voyage lasting maybe for some four standard months.

Except that with each passing moment, Michel felt less certain about the fun. He pondered, and decided it was too late now to do anything but go along.

Departure followed docking within minutes. Michel and his mother were shortly settled into modest but comfortable adjoining cabins, and the friendly young woman officer, who was evidently their assigned friend, came to take them on a tour of the parts of the ship accessible to passengers. She was full of explanations and always reassuring. That evening they all dined with the captain. The captain was a tall, gray woman with a harsh, angular face that softened briefly but remarkably when she smiled, who asked in an abstracted way if there was anything they wanted.

Ship's time had been adjusted to match local Alpine time at the longitude of the Geulincx establishment. Coincidence or not, the peculiarity of this adjustment was not lost on Michel, and did nothing to ease his growing sense of something stranger than a long space voyage getting under way.

. . . his father, his biofather whom he had never seen and did not know, was locked up in a filing cabinet somewhere aboard the *Johann Karlsen*, screaming for his son to let him out. It was up to Michel to make his way through a complexity of locks and barriers to find the trapped man, but before he could get the machinery well in hand, he realized that he had just been dreaming and was now awake. He sat up in the unfamiliar bed in the totally dark cabin, listening very intently.

Thrum.

He had never before felt the interior tug, perceived as a shadowy twisting in the bones and guts, that was a side effect of the energies released when a c-plus cannon fired close at hand. But in his spacewar books he had read descriptions enough of the effect.

Thrum. Thrum.

When he had attended, fully awake, for a half a minute, he was no longer in any doubt. He counted hours back to departure. Probably they had reached the Bottleneck already, or were very near it. They wouldn't be firing for practice here. *Thrum-thrum. Thrum.* And he thought that they would never practice-fire so steadily; it would be too hard on the vital equipment, the force manifolds in particular.

Leaving the room dark—he remembered just where his clothes lay on the floor—he slid out of bed and started to get dressed. He was three-quarters clad when his door was lightly opened, to admit from the lighted passageway the young woman officer, Ensign Schneider. She looked surprised to see him on his feet and moving.

"What's wrong, Michel?" There was a straining lightness in her voice.

"Don't you know?" he asked, mechanically, feeling sure she did. "We're under attack." He paused, one arm sleeved in his shirt, one not, sensing.

"I don't hear any—"

"Or we were. The firing stopped just now."

She was smiling at him uncertainly when Lombok stepped in from the hall behind her, wearing a robe that made him look like a little brown bird. He appeared almost elated to see that the boy was up and getting dressed. "Something wake you, Michel?"

Why were these people acting like idiots? "I want to see, Mr. Lombok. do you suppose I could just look in on the bridge? I promise I won't disturb anything."

Lombok studied him a moment, then turned to the young woman. "Ensign, why don't you just see if Mrs. Geulincx is restless too?" Then he turned away, indicating with a motion of his head that Michel should follow.

In the corridors the gravity had been reduced, just as was always done on big ships in the stories, when combat alert sounded. The soft handgrips built into the walls and overhead had become useful. He followed Lombok's fluttering brown plumage to the bridge, which, as Michel had expected, was a large, gray, brilliant room where a score of acceleration couches were almost all occupied. The faces of the occupants would have alerted anyone that something more than practice was at hand. There was one empty couch at the end of a row near where they had entered the bridge, and Lombok gestured him into it with a kind of authority that Sixtus often worked at but had never come close to attaining.

In the churchly silence Michel clambered in and

snugged the cover of the couch closed without conscious thought—it did not occur to him that he had never seen a similar mechanism before. Nor did he consider the fact that Lombok either could not see another empty couch or did not choose to look for one, but rather stayed beside Michel's. The boy's attention was already caught by the huge simulated battle presentation that filled the center of the room.

The multicolored hologram showed, like a bright tunnel zigzagging through coal, what must be a section of the Bottleneck, a jagged crevice of clear space surrounded by dark nebula. Strung irregularly through the tunnel and proceeding along it with what looked like painful slowness were green dots that—just as in the stories—showed the disposition of the human fleet. The dreadnought itself, marked by a rhythmic, tiny flash of green, was shown near the middle of the tunnel, followed by a strong rear guard.

A swarm of red dots, berserkers, came on the heels of the rear guard, which must be still heavily engaged. The dreadnought did not turn to help, nor did the strong advance guard which preceded her; they all fled for the end of the Bottleneck ahead, for open space with its infinity of pathways for their flights.

Of course the hologram was no better than a good guess. Not even the dreadnought's instruments and battle computers could very accurately interpret the specks of ships and machines seen at or near lightspeed, flickering out of normal space and back again, hiding behind dark lobes of gas or dust, obscured amid a symphony of radiation. In a little while Michel began instead to watch the battle as it was reflected in the face of the captain. In that mask of concentration he read that things were going about as well as could be expected, given the size of the enemy force that had tried to ambush them and almost succeeded.

Glancing back momentarily at the hologram, he saw a green dot of the rear guard suddenly disappear. Dots of red and green were coming and going all the time, like fireflies, as their positions were recomputed or they departed normal space and reappeared in it. But this particular disappearance was different—this green dot did not return.

He had known somehow as soon as it vanished that it was never going to come back.

An unknown number of human bodies, along with all their furniture and food supplies and good-luck charms and weaponry, had just been converted into an almost-random sleet of energy and subatomic particles. Michel swayed for a moment in his couch, not with fear but with an empathic sharing of that experience.

The mighty dreadnought fled, while the battle in the rear guard raged and swirled. The implacable red dots came on, mountains of metal that could know no fear or weariness. Michel could hear them calling faintly, with electric thoughts. Calling him to join them, and be free.

THREE

Offices on the Administration Sublevel of Moon-base tended to be deadeningly silent—or sooth-ingly so, depending upon one's viewpoint. But muted music almost always murmured in the background throughout the complex of chambers of the Secretary of Defense. Popular Western-culture melodies of the twentieth century were what he most favored.

But the Secretary, Tupelov, sitting behind his large desk with his large feet up, was not listening at the moment. "I don't take it as a hopeful sign that the kid almost fainted the first time he got into a combat couch," he said. He was a large, gross, young-looking man, who might have re-minded a historian of the early pictures of Oscar Wilde. But the resemblance was confined to phy-sique and general appearance—and, perhaps, raw intellectual ability.

"His first space flight, not to mention his first

battle," offered Lombok, who had just invited himself to take a chair. The *Johann Karlsen* had docked not twenty minutes past, and Lombok had been the first one off. "And all in the middle of the night . . . I think he's a tough kid, basically."

"You got a copy of his bioparents' genetic records?"

"They had only his mother's, at the adoption center. No name for her, but we'll run a computer search for matching records, and see what we can find."

The Secretary dropped his feet to the floor, and hitched himself into a more business-like position. "You've been with him and his mother more than four standard months now. Do they have any idea yet what's really going on?"

"I'm willing to bet the mother doesn't. And I'm almost equally willing to bet that Michel does." Lombok raised tiny fingers in a forestalling gesture. "It's nothing I can quote him as saying; nothing I can tell you he's done. It's the way he looks at me sometimes. And the things he listens very keenly to, and the things he tunes out, for example most of his mother's talk about what they'll do at the Academy."

"How about the *Karlsen*'s crew?"

"They all knew we were VIPs, and of course they speculated. I heard no speculation that sounded very close to the mark."

"So. How do you think we ought to officially break the news to our guests? And who ought to do it?"

Lombok considered. "Mamma will take it better from the highest-ranking person we can find. If you could arrange a meeting with the President—?"

"Forget that. It would take days. And he doesn't like to come up here, and I'd just as soon not take them down to Earth." Down there, the Academy would be too tantalizingly close, perhaps.

"Then you do it. I don't think it'll have too much direct effect on the kid whoever tells him. But if Mamma is badly upset for a considerable time—who knows what bad effect that might have on an eleven-year-old?"

"Okay. I'll see her in here, now." Tupelov stood up and squinted about him, trying to think of the best way to make the large office seem even more impressive to a woman from a half-settled world, who had spent much of her life almost divorced from large-scale technology. He settled for turning on the wall screens. One he adjusted to a repetitive scan of the lunar surface topside; as if the Secretary when he now and then looked up from his work did not waste a precious moment but took a turn as extra sentry. . . . There, he noticed, was the rounded top of the *Karlsen's* hull. It was high enough to be visible even over the rim of Middlehurst, the next crater over, where as late as a decade ago tourists had come to gaze at the only known live volcano on the Moon.

On the screen on the opposite wall he got an encyclopedia of impressive battle statistics flowing (old ones, but who would know?); and on the wall behind his desk he conjured up a giant image of the big blue-white marble itself, fed in from a remote pickup somewhere over the horizon on Earthside. What human, from whatever distant world, did not feel the pull et cetera of homeland et cetera, at the first sight of old Earth? Et cetera, et cetera.

He checked his appearance in a mirror, and was all set; or he would be, as soon as Lombok had let himself out by a back door. He asked that the mother be sent in first, alone, and then he met her as she entered.

"Mrs. Geulincx, very glad you could come in to see me. Please, sit down. How is everything?"

She was prettier and younger-looking than he had imagined. "My son and I are certainly being given a great welcome. But I admit I won't be able to relax until we're down on Earth."

He led her to the deluxe chair, and offered wine and smokers; she turned down both. He went to sit behind his desk. "That's what I wanted to talk to you about." Her eyes came down from his wallscreens, and he met them gravely. He let a pause lengthen considerably before going on: "As you know, Michel was chosen to come here because of some very special qualities he possesses. What you have no way of knowing . . . is that he was *not* chosen by the Academy. And not for his artistic talent, great as that must be."

She looked her total lack of comprehension at him. Tried a little smile, then let it fall.

He leaned his elbows on his desk, slumped forward, letting some of his tiredness show. "As I say, Mrs. Geulincx—may I call you Carmen? Carmen, then—there is no way you can be expected to understand. Until I explain things to you. First, humanity is not winning this war. A hundred years ago we were sure that victory was just around the corner. Fifty years ago we were still confident that the odds were with us, time was ultimately on our side. But within the past few decades we have been made to realize that neither of those hopes is true. The enemy has grown stronger, while we have not kept up the pace of weapons development. We have too often been content simply to defend ourselves, instead of going after the berserkers when we had an advantage . . . I can go into all the reasons later if you wish. For now, just take my word for it: if things go on as they have, in fifty years—in *twenty* years—there will not be an Academy to hand out scholarships to youngsters like Michel. And if Michel is still alive it may be only as a canned brain in some berserker's experimental ... are you all right? Forgive me. Here." He got up and came around the desk to her with water. The intensity of her reaction had taken him by surprise.

Carmen got her eyes in focus, sipped a little water, signaled that she now felt better, and changed her mind about the smokers. With newly frightened eyes she looked up at the Secretary through a blue, fragrant cloud, and asked him harshly: "If it was not the Academy who brought us here, then who? And why?"

"Me. Oh, I could say technically it was the Interworld War Council, but the worlds are no longer co-operating very well on anything. I could say truthfully it was Earth's government, because the plan has been approved at the very highest levels. But the plan was and is my idea."

He went back to his desk, sat down, spoke to her softly. "As to why. We are developing a new weapons system, the importance of which is hardly possible to exaggerate. The code name for it is Lancelot; I don't suppose you've ever heard it mentioned?"

She shook her head, allowing Tupelov to feel mildly reassured about security.

He went on: "I could say it's a new type of spaceship, though it's really more. Lancelot does, or will do, things that we think no berserker will ever be able to match. Because it uses as one integral component a living, willing human mind. Now this creates one problem. Most people's minds, even those of our best pilots, do not tolerate this kind of integration into a system. The subconscious as well as the conscious mind is utilized, you see. Change your mind about the wine?"

While the robot poured for her, he continued in a deliberately soothing and monotonous voice. "Some people of course did better—or less poorly—than others. Finally we developed a theoretical model of the mind that could provide a perfect match. Then we started looking for people who matched that model. It was a rare type we needed, and a difficult search. We have inspected the genetic and psychological records of almost a hundred billion living people, on Earth and on every human-colonized planet whose records we have been able to get at. Michel's records, along with many others, we found in Adoption Central, here on Earth. And out of that hundred billion, Michel is the closest match, by far, to our theoretical ideal."

"A hundred billion . . ."

Tupelov debated whether to go over to her again, and settled for coming around to the front of his desk and perching on it. "Now let me assure you at once that he won't be harmed. The tests we've brought him here for are perfectly safe."

"Oh." Relief set in. "For just a moment there I had the idea that you expected *him*—" she could smile now at her own silliness. Imagine, a skinny eleven-year-old child, her own artistic one at that, going forth to fight berserkers!

Tupelov smiled. "Once we have the hardware tuned up with an ideal personality, you see, then we can make some modifications, and choose among our trained people for the combat operators."

Carmen sipped wine, and looked at him with a face suddenly clouded by new suspicion. "There's just one thing. Why all the mystery? Why didn't you simply tell us the truth on Alpine?"

"Alpine is a dangerous planet, Carmen, in more than one way. I mean it's hard to keep a secret from the berserkers, once even a few people on Alpine know it. I don't mean to insult your compatriots, but there it is."

"Goodlife." Her mouth made a little grimace over the word. "The Alpine government is always warning about berserker-lovers, telling everyone to keep military matters secret. But Sixtus always says those goodlife stories are just a device to boost morale. Though I never quite understood why they should have that effect."

"I have access to a lot more information on the subject than Sixtus is likely to see. Take it from me. Michel would have been in real danger if word had leaked out about why he was really being brought to Earth."

Carmen's eyes were suddenly wide. "When the berserkers attacked us in the Bottleneck. Did that have anything to do with—?"

"Did they know anything about Michel? I really don't know." He tried a reassuring smile. "Fortunately you came through it." Actually there had been an additional reason for not telling the Alpine government what was up: in their own somewhat desperate situation vis-a-vis the berserkers, they might have declared Michel a valuable national resource, or something along that line, and forbidden his export. Not that they would then have been able to use him, of course. The right human operator was only half of Lancelot, and to develop the other half had been the work of decades even for mighty Earth.

"I'd like to talk to Michel now, Carmen, fill him in on what's going on. I just wanted to make sure that you were filled in first." The woman nodded slowly. Tupelov was thinking that this was going better, much better, than it might have gone.

When he signaled the outer office, Michel entered immediately, looking as Lombok had described him, and wearing casual clothes grown somewhat too small. Tupelov saw that the boy had already acquired a chunk of soft Earth pine, which nestled like an angular egg in one of his hands; a little carving knife was in the other. Michel looked silently from one adult to the other, his own somewhat pinched face unreadable.

As if welcoming a distinguished adult, the Secretary got up and showed him to a chair. If he'd had any forethought he would have had a softer drink than wine laid in.

"I've just been explaining to your mother," he began, while shaking hands, "that your trip to the Academy is going to have to be delayed." He glanced, as charmingly as possible, back to the woman. "Oh, we'll see to it that he gets one." They would, too, if Michel and the Academy both lasted long enough. "But it might not be for a year or more."

He turned back to the boy, who did not look in the least stunned. "Michel, we have some space suits and other equipment that we'd like your help in testing." Tupelov was ready to explain that he was not joking.

"I know," Michel answered unexpectedly. He was gazing now with a curious frown at the wallscreen on the Secretary's right, the one unrolling old and jumbled data. "That thing's not working, is it?"

Tupelov turned to the screen and back to the boy. He stared. "How do you know?"

"If you mean about the screen, it's all . . ." Michel made a helpless gesture with one thin arm, throwing away something beyond fixing. "I guess the hardware's all right—almost all right—but the figures are—funny."

"And how did you know about the suits? The things we want you to test?"

"Oh, I don't know what they are. But I know it's you who really brought me. I mean that whole fleet wasn't doing anything else, as far as I could see. It came to Alpine just for us—for me—and brought us straight back here. And what use could *I* be to you, except for some kind of test, or an experiment?"

Carmen's eyes were rounding as she listened, to this one-in-a-hundred-billion being who had somehow turned out to be her son. Before either adult could reply, a communicator sounded on Tupelov's desk, and he bent over into its zone of privacy to answer. When he straightened up again he said, "They're ready for us to come to the lab and take a look at Lancelot. Shall we?"

In a chamber not far below the surface they first confronted Michel with the thing they wanted him to wear. The chamber was big enough for football, and its edges were crowded with improbable devices. Its massively girdered ceiling was relatively low, only five meters or so above the floor, and brilliant with pleasant lights.

At one edge of the vast cleared space in the center of the room, the thing they wanted him to test was waiting, suspended from the overhead and looking vaguely like a parachute harness. Only vaguely. Actually Michel was reminded not so much of military hardware as of costumes from a school play when he was seven. In the play there had been crowns, and gauzy robes, and for one actor a magic wand to wave. Here no rods of power were visible, but when they had him standing right under the suspended harness someone turned something on, and immediately there were robes in profusion, trailing away from the fragmentary suit across the otherwise empty floor. He recognized it as a great web of some kind of forcefields. The fields seemed to wave in a manner that suggested they were being driven by a racing wind, and after thirty meters or so they vanished, into their own self-contained distance. Michel understood that the waves and folds were really patterns generated in the eye, which wanted to see solidity where there was no more than a certain interference with passing light.

He exchanged smiles with his mother, who stood very near him, holding the arm of Ensign Schneider and looking nervous. Then, while murmuring replies to the questions of the technicians who now began to fit the first straps of the harness to him, he turned his head to look at the mirage of field patterns. He let his eyes and mind play with them, seeking out reality beneath.

Tupelov had quietly excused himself, and was now in an adjoining room where some of his science department heads and other important people were watching the fitting via wallscreen; the idea was that the technicians could get on with these preliminaries better if not too much rank was in the way.

Entering the small room, the Secretary acknowledged greetings with a nod, took one look at the screen, and asked the assembly bluntly, "What do you think?" He knew how premature his question was; but he knew also that if he didn't keep prodding some of these people they'd let things drag on forever. Also an observer from the President's staff was in the group, and the Secretary wanted to be sure the President understood just who was trying to hurry things along.

One of the scientists, a bearded man whose bulging forehead made him rather look the part, shrugged. "Hardly seems the warrior type."

Tupelov stared. "You mean no big muscles, no

steely glare, no commanding presence? You know none of that means shit in terms of the performance we require."

The scientist looked back boldly, though it no doubt cost him an effort. "But that's all we have as yet to evaluate, hey?"

The President's observer, who had arrived from Earth within the hour, interrupted. "But, Mr. Secretary. What exactly *is* it that makes Michel the ideal candidate for this job? I mean, I've been shown on paper how well he matches the desired profile. but what is this genetic makeup of his supposed to produce in the way of action?"

"All right. First of all, you can see they're taking their time out there with what looks like a routine job of fitting on some straps. It's really much more than that. There are several powerful kinds of psychic feedback involved, even at the minimum power settings they're using. Most people, you and I included, would already be screaming and trying to get away if we were standing where Michel is now."

The slight, pale-haired figure out there kept turning his head, looking around. That was the only sign that anything might be bothering him.

"But surely," said the President's woman, "what he has is not just—stolidity, or a high pain threshold?"

Tupelov violently shook his head. "One, that kid has as great an affinity for machines as any engineer we've ever tested—so great it gets spooky sometimes. Two, his Intelligence Spectrum goes across the board in high numbers—though not the very highest. Again, an IS like that is ideal. Three, he is simply off the scale in human empathy.

"So far, we might have found a number of good candidates without leaving Earth, where we have ten billion or so citizens to choose from. But we also needed, and Michel also has, an awesome psychological toughness and stability—you might call that stolidity. I suppose. Now what does all this add up to? Well, I've seen an independent evaluation of his measurements, by one of Earth's great psychologists who has no idea what we're up to. She thought the subject might be expected to found a great religion—except for one thing: the leadership potential is simply not there."

The lady from the President's office tilted her head to one side. "You make that sound like an advantage too, Mr. Secretary."

"Oh, it is." Tupelov bit at a thumbnail, for the moment looking like the village idiot. "You don't yet understand the powers that Lancelot will eventually bestow upon its operator."

After a moment he went on: "My own bet might be for Michel to become a great saint in someone else's church—except we come back to that affinity for mechanism of all kinds, which is simply too overwhelming not to play a great part in his life."

"He doesn't tinker, does he? I thought he carved."

"Oh, it'll come out eventually—it has to. Incidentally, as we were walking over here, I asked him why carving instead of some other art. And he answered without having to think: Carvings last, he said. They're something that lasts."

The fitters kept gleefully assuring him that he had most of the suit on, now—as if just getting it on were some sort of an ordeal, which, when he thought about it, he supposed might be true for most people. There were all sorts of signals feeding back from the intricate forcefields into his brain—but he could ride the current, he could keep his balance, even if he had not yet discovered any way to steer. Later he would ask about controls—for now, he had enough to do.

Michel was distracted from his learning by the entrance into the vast room of someone much different from any human being he had ever met before. The newcomer came rolling upon tall wheels in a series of three boxes connected almost like cars of a toy train, and of a size that would have been convenient to ride on. The assembly was superficially like some of the freight-robots that from time to time appeared here in the background. But the boxes' shapes were all wrong for ordinary freight, and the path of the self-guided conveyance was not deferential enough by several centimeters as it cut across the path of two technicians walking. Nor did the people working with Michel react as to a mere machine's arrival. Their hands paused and their heads turned.

The train rolled to a stop nearby. "Hi, kid," said a casual voice from the front box, its timbre confirming Michel's guess that the occupant was an adult male.

"Hi." He'd heard and read of a few people, in very bad shape physically, who preferred artificial bodies of this style to those of a more humanoid shape—which could never really, Michel supposed, be human enough.

The voice said: "I've tried on that thing you're wearing. Doesn't feel too good, hey?"

"I don't mind it."

"Great! I *do* mind it, but I can wear it. So maybe, if you have any questions as the work goes on, I can help you find an answer." The tone was infinitely more confident than the words.

"There don't seem to be any controls at all," Michel remarked.

After a pause the voice from the box asked him: "Does your body have any?"

"I see."

"Kid—Michel—what you're wrapped up in there is biotechnology carried to the ultimate. Way ahead of this little circus train I ride around in usually. By the way, my name is Frank."

There was an interruption; the technicians were ready to turn on something else. They did, and with the altered flow of power Michel's perceptions shifted. For him, the meters of solid lunar rock and regolith above his head became transparent. This was followed by another and even more startling transformation, as what had been the black and starry sky turned into something else, an infinite cave draped by innumerable lines and veils of force. It was a shining mansion whose limitlessness would have frightened him if he could ever have felt fear at anything so impersonal. Slowly his awe passed, and he discovered that he could turn away from that new universe and close the Moon overhead once more, willing his perceptions back to his immediate surroundings in the hangar.

In a moment he reached out in a different direction. Two underground levels below, a pair of officers who moved as if they thought themselves very important were talking as they walked together. "The astragalus," said one, "is one of the proximal bones of the tarsus; and it was used in ancient times in randomizing—"

Distraction: Eleven-point-six and a little more kilometers away, a large-sized pebble was falling at meteoric speed toward the lunar surface. An eyeblink later some automated defense machine had taken aim and obliterated the pebble in midflight; a mere twitch in a single cell of the complex electronic organism that comprised the main defenses of Moonbase.

Distraction: Somewhere on Moonbase's deepest

level, behind doors with the gravest security warnings on them, a hologram-model of the galaxy was packed all round its Core with white blank volumes representing the uncharted and unknown. Amid these a fanatically precise technician was creating an electronic label for something that looked vaguely like a geodesic sphere made out of toothpicks. The label said merely; TAJ. It was something built on a scale of size above that of even the most enormous stars.

Distraction: Something stirred with a life of its own, inside the lower abdomen of the youngest of the female technicians nearby, as two of them reached up to fit Michel with the blinding circlet of what looked like his crown. And even in the heavily shielded boxes of the canned man Michel could detect organic stirrings, peristalsis.

Distraction: A great buzz, which he soon realized must be the thermal motion of air molecules about him. In a moment, he had learned to tune it out.

When the fitting was over, some twenty minutes after it had begun, he emerged from the helm and harness blinking at the odd version of reality that he had accepted for eleven years with so little thought. He would never be the same.

FOUR

THE LITTLE PERSONNEL PRINTOUT WITH TEMESVAR EL-
lison in block capitals across its top went skitter-
ing over the surface of the desk, tossed by
Lombok's nimble little fingers. Tupelov's big, soft,
nail-bitten ones fumbled it up on the second try.

"His biomother," Lombok announced, in la-
conic explanation. "Genetic pattern fits too well
to leave any real doubt. And she was on Alpine at
the right time."

"So?" One glance at each side and Tupelov had
read the printout, which outlined Elly Temesvar's service career from enrollment to the time
of her resignation approximately eleven years
ago. "Doesn't ring any . . . oh. Wait. This is the
girl who was with Marcus, on the second sighting
of the Taj. When he went right through part of it
trying to shake off a berserker. So she's also
Michel's—"

Breaking off in mid-sentence, the Secretary

looked at the printout again, executing with unconscious perfection an actor's double-take.

"Exactly," put in Lombok. "It looks like Frank Marcus is almost certainly his father. I'll do a genetic pattern study on that too, to make sure."

Tupelov signed agreement. "But very quietly. Do it yourself. Marcus ... hasn't seen this yet, of course."

"Of course not. No reason to think that he has any suspicion of the relationship. Or that Michel has either."

"The dates all mesh ... so she got pregnant on that mission. But it says nothing here about her being pregnant when they returned to base—no reason why it should, I suppose—*or* about pregnancy being a reason when she resigned a few months later. It just quotes her as saying she had, quote, 'lost interest in her career,' unquote. Well, after six months alone with Marcus I can understand anyone quitting."

"If you'll note," said Lombok, "Alpine was the first place they put in at, on their way back to their original base, CORESEC. It would seem she just had the pregnancy terminated at the first place she reasonably could, and never mentioned it to the service doctors."

"Yeah ... yeah ... I want to think about this. We'll keep it very quiet for now."

"Agreed."

"But you're standing there looking at me, Angelo, as if you want permission to do something."

"I think I ought to go see just what Elly Temesvar is up to now. Talk to her. Maybe even bring her to Moonbase, if I can, on some pretext."

"Why?"

"What she is will have some bearing on what Michel is, and will become. And it strikes me that from her service record alone we just don't know very much about her."

"We know her present address?"

"On Earth. At least she was there last year. She agreed to take part in a routine census-sampling then. Someplace called the Temple of the Final Savior."

"Sounds like a religion. I never heard of it, though."

"Nor I. There are always new ones; they come and go."

Tupelov was silent for a few seconds. He put a finger in his mouth, took it out, picked at the cuticle. "I'm not sure we ought to bring her up here just now. It might only draw attention."

"I would like to have permission to do so, at my discretion. After that ambush at the Bottleneck, in such force, we have to assume that the enemy knows something of Michel's importance, and that he's here. Then word will soon reach their local goodlife friends, on Earth. It's not impossible that they'll also know that Temesvar's his mother. The records in the adoption center are supposedly quite secure, but it's on Alpine."

"Yeah. That place. All right, Angelo, if you think you must."

Michel had the feeling that things were being rushed.

He had been on Moonbase just a little longer than one standard day, and this was the second time he had put on Lancelot, and now he was wearing it as his only protection as he rode a large platform elevator up to the airless, frozen night-side surface. The hundred or so adults who rode with him, military people and scientists and technicians, wore spacesuits, all of them . . . well, almost all. Frank, as he said, carried his own spacesuit with him wherever he went.

Frank's little train of boxes was at Michel's right as they rode up, and at his left stood Edmond Iyenari, head of the scientific team, whose engagingly ugly eyes kept studying Michel keenly from behind their faceplate as the elevator rose.

"All right, Michel?" Dr. Iyenari asked.

"All right."

"I was sure you would be."

The air was going from around them now. They had told him that Lancelot would provide him with all the air he needed, all the oxygen, to be exact, and he had no real doubt that they were right. Michel still felt perfectly comfortable as, with dropping pressure, the furled stuff of Lancelot around him crackled a little, a sound suggesting stiff paper wings. The fields were almost invisible and impalpable, and he had no sensation of being sealed or encased in anything.

A medical doctor, one of the group of nearby people all watching Michel with tremendous casualness, said, "You're still breathing." It was somewhere between a comment and a question.

"Yes," said Michel, and immediately became self-conscious about the fact. There was still air pressure, or what felt just like air pressure, in his breathing passages, and evidently pressure of some kind capping his nose and mouth to keep whatever was in his lungs from bursting out. Earlier he had been given a brief explanation, which he only partly understood, of how Lancelot's fields, through a thousand painless piercings of his skin, could supply his body with what it needed and take its wastes away to be processed and reused. Now he discovered that he could effortlessly cease breathing if he thought about it, and the reflex to start did not take hold.

A moment later, and he forgot about his body. Above, huge doors were opening, and beyond them shone the stars.

On Alpine, it was possible now and then to see a star. There were days, sometimes even weeks when a nebular window opened and a fingernail-sized patch of the galaxy shone through. When that happened, people tended to gather outdoors at night and point.

The more peaceful stretches of Michel's journey from Alpine to Moonbase had afforded him his first real chance to get a look at what was still commonly called the Milky Way. But looking at the stars through a screen or even a cleared port had been seeing them at one remove. It had not been like this. As the elevator now eased to a stop, flush with the lunar surface, Earth and Sun were both below the horizon, and from edge to edge the sky seemed to be filled with stars.

It was not terrifying for one reason only—it was so utterly remote.

Squinting a little, Michel raised his right arm to point. He remembered to draw breath before he spoke, so his words would come out clearly, and what functioned as a radio transmitter in Lancelot would convey them to the others' suit receivers. He asked, pointing, "What's that?"

"You mean the three stars in a row?" Iyenari responded doubtfully. "That's the belt of Orion— the Hunter, we call him sometimes. You've heard something about our constellations?"

"Not the three stars." Michel jabbed the sky with a forefinger trailing parabolic whorls of silver gauze. "Farther over there." The thing he saw was almost dazzling, and contained colors that he could not remember having seen before. Words to describe it were not easily come by.

"Taurus? The Bull . . ."

Abruptly Michel realized that the others, looking with normal and unaided eyes, could not see
the thing at all. The dazzle was all in short wavelengths of radiation that only Lancelot allowed his
eyes to see. As preparations for the day's first tests
continued, Michel glanced back from time to time
at the object in the sky. Gradually he learned how
to dim the dazzle reaching his eyes, and at the
same time to magnify the source somewhat. A
ragged-looking cloud of gases of some kind, a gi-
gantic explosion still in progress but frozen by its
own vast scale to seeming immobility. How far
away? Some hundreds of lightyears, at a guess.

Centered on the platform of the risen elevator
there extended a plain of fused basalt several hec-
tares in extent, flat as a parking lot amid a gently
rolling sea of lunar regolith whose waves and cups
reached in every direction eight or ten kilometers
before rising to make the interior rim of a broad
impact crater whose name Michel had not been
told. Poles had been erected around the platform,
in a square a few score meters on a side, roofed
and walled by a network of some kind of rope or
wire. The holes in the net, Michel noticed, were
just too small to allow an object the size of his
own body to pass through. The construction, he
thought, might have been borrowed from the court
of some game in which a large bouncing ball was
used.

Around Michel a hundred suits of space armor
groaned faintly, making adjustments to the topside cold and vacuum. Their wearers, mostly busy
with other matters, did not appear to notice. When
Michel himself moved, he could hear Lancelot
faintly crackling, weak spasms across the audio
spectrum.

He asked Dr. Iyenari about the crackling, and
tried to absorb an answer completely unintelligi-

ble, a few words of physics tied up in math. Maybe someone he would have learned enough in school to understand that. Meanwhile it seemed preferable to try to feel out an answer for himself.

"Ready to give it a try?" Tupelov's tall, suited figure was towering over him. The Secretary always spoke to Michel as to a respected equal.

"Sure." Below, while Michel was being robed in a tight-fitting gym suit of bright orange and then in Lancelot, they had discussed briefly what was to be tried today, simple free flight in space. As the thought returned that things were being rushed a bit, bright lights suddenly flooded the basalt area. Michel knew another momentary dazzle before Lancelot scaled down the radiation impinging from the sources directly into his eyes. Rushing things, but they must have their reasons, good ones, because it was certain that neither Tupelov nor any of the others here wanted their pet subject to get hurt.

Now technicians had surrounded Michel closely, to fit him with additional Lancelot-components. Here came tube-shaped things and egg-shaped things and cubes. All vanished somehow into Lancelot's fields, leaving the gauzy wings and robes no more substantial-looking than before. None of the additions seemed to add up to any more weight or bulk.

Michel let his attention drop away. Four levels below where he stood, and maybe a dozen kilometers to the lunar east, his mother was conversing, brightly and eagerly, with another lady, a vice-president of the Academy. His mother thought it was a coincidence that an Academy official, a real one this time, had just happened to be on Moonbase at this hour with some time available to talk. . . .

Dr. Iyenari was speaking, for the benefit of some

recorders. "Today, we want to begin by using only a simple tidal collector in a forcepower mode. We'll charge with that continuously, while using a prestored charge for the maneuvers. Only elementary maneuvers are planned for the first trial with this subject. He will rise from the ground to a height of two or three meters, under the nets, and make a controlled descent. When we have a successful trial up to that point, we'll decide how much farther we want to go today."

Michel knew that Lancelot had a backup power supply too, a hydrogen lamp that as far as he could guess was several times as large as it needed to be, whatever the designers' reasoning. The lamp rode somewhere in the haze extending for a meter or two to the rear of Michel's shoulder blades. It existed now the scientists had told him, only in a quasimaterial form, the molecules of its once-solid structure represented by a patterning of forces. What would have been forces in an unmodified lamp were now no more than sketches of something more abstract and subtle still, despite which the hydrogen lamp kept right on working anyway. Of course, as one of the scientists had said, solid matter was itself no more than a patterning, of something that Michel thought he could now almost perceive, at moments, when he reached for it in the proper way with his new senses. . . .

Having run his own check on the power lamp, a check that he himself did not understand very well and could not have explained to an engineer (who would not have understood it either), Michel forgot that it was there. Turning round slowly in place, as was required of him in the last stages of today's fitting, he noticed that the far slopes of the crater wall were turning into a sort of grandstand, acquiring a considerable population of suited humans and their choice machines. Some were scientific observers. Many, he realized, zooming his perceptions in among them here and there, were guards of one kind and another.

"Step over here now, please, Michel."

They led him to where a great yellow X, micro-metrically exact in its dimensions, had been marked on the pavement. His feet in the soft-soled shoes that they had given him were positioned carefully at its center. From somewhere a fragment of his mother's voice, recognizable by tone and breathing pattern, came through the background noise of all kinds. Still four levels down, she was talking with cheerful animation about Art.

What would it be like to hold a piece of wood in his hand, a knife in Lancelot's, and carve? Entrancing as this speculation was, he had only a moment for it before voices were once more demanding his attention.

"All right, Michel?"

"Yes. All right."

The nearest other person stood some ten meters from the yellow X, the nearest machine a little farther still.

"There'll be no countdown or anything, just whenever you're ready. Can you get off the ground now? Slowly. Don't worry if nothing moves just at first. . . ."

He never doubted that in Lancelot he would be enabled to move as he had never moved before. There were, though, certain other problems. Just at the moment when his slipper-light shoes were losing their tenure on the pavement, an alarming potential of sideways acceleration threatened to achieve reality and almost did. Michel shied like a novice bike-rider from an incipient fall. His re-action was just a little too strong. At the moment of rising from the ground, he lurched minutely to-ward the nets (whose purpose he now thought he understood) that were waiting for him in the opposite direction. Around him, voices muttered, people tried to suppress excitement and triumph so that he should not be distracted by it.

One voice, tense, encouraging, spoke to him openly, but he did not need that voice either and he tuned it out. He needed no encouragement and he realized now that there were no helpful instructions anyone could give him. Probably no one had ever *thought* this way before. Michel, drifting above the surface gently, experimented, trying to understand that first unexpected sideways surge. It was something, he thought, deriving from the motion of the Moon itself beneath him. Dimly, when he made the effort, he could now begin to feel the great slow harmonies of rotation, of revolution riding revolution as the Moon's track rode that of Earth and the Earth marched with the Sun toward some constellation never to be seen in Alpine's skies.

That one monotonous voice continued to encourage him, as if its owner thought it was a lifting force. Spaceborne, Michel turned slowly in the bright lights, close beneath the wide-stretched upper net. Gauze robes swirled from him as he turned, and lifted faces ringed him in. The school play. Never in his life before or since had he been the center of so much attention, until now. Maybe they would all soon applaud. . . .

He raised his right arm, a gesture from the play, and with comfortable and sensitive fingers touched the soft toughness of the net, which someone had told him was three meters from the deck. Avidly following the movement of his arm went the aimings, adjustments, swallowings of cameras and recorders, so different in their working from human eyes and minds.

Join us. Be—

Probably the calling did not come from berserkers, or not from berserkers alone. Be. Something. Something that could perhaps be contained in the word *machine*; there seemed to be no human word that really fit.

No. In the manner of an easy, floating swimmer, he guided himself all the way across the top of the cabled cage. The voice that had been talking to him all along now registered as Tupelov's, and still it went on, excited and encouraging. It was starting to give orders now, and Michel listened to it, enough to get the gist of what it wanted. Obediently he made his way completely across the cage and back, then came down again just where he had started.

As soon as his feet were planted once more on the yellow X, a dozen people closed in upon him with a rush. Frank Marcus was there as soon as anyone, and Michel leaned on one of the rolling boxes, putting a little distance between himself and the suited people who came crowding on his other side. As soon as the first burst of questioning was over, and the leaders had turned away from Michel to confer among themselves, Frank remarked, "First time I tried it, Michel, I damn near went through the net. So did the only other person who's ever got this far with it. We were all more or less expecting you'd do the same. They said it would be better not to warn you, just to let you find your own way. Maybe they were right."

"Who was the only other person?"

"Another pilot. He hit the net, and then went crazy."

Michel said, "Just when you were starting to take off, something dragged you sideways."

"Yeah." Frank's hardware was all utterly motionless, and Michel knew somehow that the man was listening very attentively.

Michel stuttered and fell silent. He didn't know how to begin to tell what he had done to avoid the deflection, how he had managed the steady flight; he didn't know if the right words or even the right language had ever been invented. And it shook him somehow that Frank, an adult well ahead of other adults in this line of business, just stood there waiting patiently to hear.

On that first day of space trials he made two more successful flights, performing maneuvers of gradually increasing complexity. He wasn't tired when they called a halt.

For the next two days he toured Moonbase with his mother and Ensign Schneider, carved a little, rested when they urged him to, though he still hadn't done anything that made him feel tired. He played, half-heartedly, security guards in view, with children whose parents worked at the base. Meanwhile he was told that the first flight tests were being evaluated, and some minor changes being made in Lancelot. Then he was once more riding the giant elevator to the surface in his orange gym suit and gauzy immaterial robes. Frank Marcus, riding up beside him once again, had this time been transformed by being put into what he called his own flight suit, a single ovoid box.

On the surface the first thing Michel noticed was that a slow-dawning Sun had fired some distant crater-rims with silver. The second change he saw was that the cabled cage had been removed.

Tupelov's visored face smiled down at Michel in yet another careful inspection. Then the man awkwardly turned away. Suited cripples, the lot of them, Michel thought suddenly, and had a sudden feeling of kinship with Frank.

The squat metal ovoid beside Michel was beginning to look like the drawing of a speeding bullet, or of a large artillery shell perhaps. A striated blurring grew in the surrounding space, as careful technicians robed Frank in his own version of Lancelot.

When Frank next spoke, it was with his radio turned off, so that the sound came to Michel only, through the contact between the fields they wore. "Kid, I think they're rushing us a little."

With a mental order, Michel cut off his own radio transmission. "Me too," he answered.

"You feel all right about it?"

"I don't know. I guess so. They haven't told me yet exactly what they want today."

"They don't tell you a lot, do they? It's gonna be elementary combat maneuvers. I've tried it once before. They'll fly some kind of drone device out across the crater and you and I'll take turns trying to catch up with it and attack."

"Oh. What kind of weapons?"

"Remember what I said when you asked me about controls?"

"Oh. Yeah." Michel considered what the natural weapons of his body had to be. Fists and feet would have to be included, and he supposed he could do some damage with his teeth. There had to be more to it than that. He would find out when the time came.

The order came for Frank, who was to fly first, to take his place at the starting point, the now-familiar yellow X. Someone announced that the drone was ready now. In the past few days Michel had seen a good many of the machines at Moonbase and he had no difficulty in recognizing the basic type of the flying drone: a powered hoister, many times stronger in lifting capacity than any single human muscular system could be, though certainly not speedy in comparison with other transport devices. Its small engine was a miniature of the type used for centuries in spacecraft when traversing gravitational fields—it worked by warping gravity in its interior, allowing its own fields to grip and haul against the stuff of space itself.

A flash of red light and a radio tone signaled that launch was imminent. Then the semi-robotic drone ran forward a few steps, on six extremely stable though awkward-looking legs. It lifted, limbs folding back at once against its blunt mass of a body, a little bigger than a man's. Faster than a man could run it flew, just off the deck, heading straight in the direction of the crater's most distant curve of wall.

Frank's start signal sounded, and the blunt bullet of his housing rose in pursuit at once. His take-off was skewed badly at the start; people hit the deck to give him room. But he got his motion quickly under control even as he accelerated after the fleeing drone. In the spotlights that followed him across the plain his gauze webs looked like a brief trail of rocket exhaust against the starry black above.

The drone clumsily sought to evade Frank, but he closed with it rapidly, now hurtling like a missile. It accelerated also, but to no avail. Impact against the far wall of the crater seemed imminent, and observers nearest the threatened point were scrambling for revetments when Frank overtook his prey. Like enormous extensions of his short metal arms, his Lancelot's immaterial talons closed on the target. His field-web flared, like the wing feathers of some giant raptor braking. At the moment of capture the target gave up, shutting itself off. In a slower, laden flight, Frank wheeled it round and bore it back beneath him to the basalt pad.

"Get the idea, Michel?" This from Tupelov.

"I think so."

"We'll go once more with Marcus, first, if he's still . . . How're you doing, Colonel?"

"Ready." Michel could detect the mutual dislike in both voices, and in Frank's an extra strain that must be due to wearing Lancelot.

A few minutes' delay went by, for reorganization and to give Frank a rest. Michel teetered on his toes, ready to fly, wishing they'd let him. Then at last the flying drone lunged away again, and again Frank went racing after it. This time he made a better takeoff.

For this trial the drone had been programmed to take defensive action, and although the point of interception was almost the same, what followed was not. An explosive struggle flared at the focus of all the observers' eyes and cameras. Michel, trying to watch, found that he had taken off without realizing it, and was again drifting easily three meters above the deck, looking over a wall of suited adult bodies.

At the focal point of a dozen spotlights, the distant combatants were down, amid a splashing of quick-settling dust. The drone, struggling to escape, was allowed only defensive action. Frank was not so limited. His aggression took form in an extension of his Lancelot's fields, forming what looked like a flat paw of enormous size. As quickly as an arm could swing, it struck at the drone, pounding the powerful lifter down out of space and against the rocks. Dust and gravel flew, but the drone bounced up at once, still struggling to escape.

Gray, tenuous-looking limbs extending themselves from his Lancelot, Frank grappled with his prey. Both of them were down on the surface now, spinning in a dance made stately by the slow parabolic sheets of dust and gravel that their movements launched in the low gravity. Frank's forcefields, like a wrestler's arms, clamped the drone's machinery against his own. In the background of Michel's attention, timers continued to spin their digits: fifteen seconds now since Frank had launched, twenty seconds—

Three seconds more and Frank had the grip he wanted, despite the drone's six wrestling limbs. One more second after that, and he had delivered the finishing blow.

In the drone's electronic nervous system something snapped, and this time it did not bounce up from rock. A moment later Frank, his own hardware evidently a little bent somewhere inside, was in limping flight back toward the starting marks, his inert trophy suspended beneath his shimmering bullet-shape as though in great translucent claws.

This time, as soon as he had landed, people and support machines surrounded him, inflating a temporary air bubble. In a moment the top of his box had been opened. Michel, now standing on the deck again and peering between suited bodies, caught a glimpse of human flesh inside the box. He saw what appeared to be bearded facial skin, mushroom pale in the overhead lights, running in a narrow strip across the front of a titanium skull.

Something—could it have been something in the attitude of that mostly-metallic head?—made Michel turn then and look in the opposite direction. In the rear circle of watchers there stood a woman in a suit no different from the rest, a woman Michel now remembered having seen at various Moonbase times and places without having given her any particular thought. She was young, and her skin was very dark, her lips full as if she pouted. But she did not pout. She merely stood there looking with the rest at Frank, but her gaze as the canned man came partially into view was much more intent and very different from the rest.

Someone came to Michel with a question, and he soon forgot about the woman. The maintenance operation on Frank was quickly completed, and Frank was rolling to a place beside Michel again.

With radio transmitter off, Frank asked him, "They tell you what they want now?"

"Only that I'm going up next. I figure they want me to chase the drone a few times."

"Yeah. Then after that they're going to have you and me spar a little."

"Spar?"

"A make-believe fight. Well, not quite make-believe. Ever see boxers, just practicing? Like that, heavily padded gloves. Don't sweat it, nobody here wants you to get hurt, believe me."

The idea of fighting against Frank seemed somewhat unreal. But the part about nobody wanting him, Michel, to get hurt was so obviously and logically true that it took most of the alarm out of the prospect of a fight.

A fight. He had once or twice been through angry, childish scuffles with playmates. Once another boy had punched him in the lip, made his mouth bleed . . . but of course that was all before Lancelot, long before. And so it had really happened to someone else. . . .

"Ready, Michel? Let's see if you can catch the drone."

He walked on poised feet to the starting mark, and there thought readiness for flight, so that his toes just rested on the mark. A new drone had been pushed forward, and now on command lurched into flight toward the distant crater wall. Michel snapped himself back from a brief reverie, into complete attention on the job at hand. He willed himself after the drone, and with the willing saw the yellow X-mark fall from beneath his feet and fly away behind him. Arms half-extended, he leaned forward, thinking flight. Far ahead the drone receded, dragging spotlights with it.

Think flight, pursuit, and overtaking, and now the patch of brilliance centered on the drone grew larger, nearer. Think flight, speed, catching up ... it had very little to do with imagination. Imagine yourself jumping up from your chair and running across the room, and you stayed seated.

He could feel that his commands to Lancelot were fumbling, groping things, only beginning to find out their true paths. But in the main they worked. Adjusting his vision now, he saw the closing drone in a far wider spectrum than that of light. He could have counted the scratches on its surface at hundreds of meters' distance, and gauged the depth of each.

All this in the five seconds following his takeoff, and in a few seconds more he had caught up with the speeding drone. Effortlessly matching its course, he approached it from above and spread his arms. His own child's arms were far too short to encircle the metal body, but at his wish Lancelot reached out field-arms three meters long, tailored to be just the proper size. Michel closed his own arms, and sensed the captured weight as Lancelot's grip clamped on. With that the drone went dead, became sheer hurtling weight, trying to fall. Lancelot's power effortlessly coped. Michel's own flight path did not dip by a centimeter from where he wanted it to be.

Spontaneous cheers broke from the small crowd of watchers as Michel flew in a wide curve with his catch. He dumped the dead drone—carefully— at Tupelov's feet just seventeen seconds after it had been launched. He couldn't remember what

Frank's time on his first flight had been, against an unresisting target.

Again there was a short break for rest, for evaluation, for many questions. Then Tupelov, beaming, announced: "Michel, we're going to have Colonel Marcus fly out now, as fast as he can, and take evasive action. Think you can catch him?"

"Yes," said Michel, and immediately thought to himself: That was too blunt. I should talk in a way to make them all feel a little more comfortable with me. They were going to be less and less comfortable, he expected, as things went on.

Seconds later, he and Frank were both on their starting marks again. Then Frank was off, precisely on time, lifting more smoothly than before. Michel, as his own timer zeroed, found himself fractionally hanging back, responding to a sudden internal urge to make what promised to be a dull chase more exciting. Then he released himself, imagining vaguely an arrow flying from a bow.

The soft-looking waves of the Moon's surface were flickering underneath him once again. As Michel closed, Frank turned, trying to evade. Now just ahead of them a high portion of the crater's rim glowed in an uneven line with the new day's silver fire. Michel followed. Frank turned again, and yet again, a darting, last-second maneuver this time, but it did him no good. The bullet of his ovoid body came underneath Michel precisely, and the boy slapped it with the field-extensions of both his hands.

Frank grunted an honest congratulation. Again there was jubilation on the radio. They flew back to the pad together, Michel slowing his own pace to that of the tired flyer beside him. Then, this time carefully tamping momentum back into the reservoirs where Lancelot could hold it stored, Michel dropped back onto the basalt surface.

The Secretary once more loomed above him, beaming. "That was very good, Michel. That was excellent. Do you think you could go faster still? But remember, stay below the crater rim. The defense computers get the electronic jitters sometimes; we don't want you showing up on their detectors."

"I think so. Yes, I could." A little more modest and thoughtful, that was it, a better answer this time. Actually, where the limits of Lancelot lay he did not know. He did not have them yet in sight, let alone within his grasp.

Tupelov turned. "Colonel Marcus?"

The metal box said on radio: "I was going all out, or very nearly."

"Are you good for another run? Or—"

"Yeah, let's get on with it. I'll let you know if I can't."

"All right, pursuit again this run. This time Michel will be the target."

"What the hell good is that? How'm I supposed to catch him? I can't."

Ten seconds of cool silence. "Very well, Colonel, Michel pursues again. All right with you, Michel?"

"All right."

"You take some defensive action, Marcus. Gently."

"Yes sir." Michel heard the voice-sound alter as Frank went off radio again. "Hear that, kid? When you catch me, we'll spar. You try to knock me right into the ground. I'll slap back at you."

"I hear."

"Come at me hard. He says gently, but if all this horsing around is going to prove anything, we've got to start being a little serious about it. We may get jarred, but neither of us is going to be really hurt, we're too well shielded inside these things."

Inside? What things? It took Michel a moment to remember.

Back to the starting marks. This time Frank, evidently drawing on some reserve of strength, got off even faster than before. Michel flew on his own timer's dot, and overtaking Frank took him no longer than in the previous trial. But at the last moment before interception, Frank's blurred shape changed course more sharply than Michel had yet seen—and then, just as Michel's grasping fields were closing, changed again.

For the first time since his first takeoff Michel was not in complete control of what his Lancelot was doing. In a spinning turn, he clawed for a grip on the great metal ovoid, and felt only the other Lancelot's contending forces, trying to get away. In the next moment Frank surprised him, managing to knock the grip of one of Michel's forcefield arms away.

Spinning in a paralysis caused more by the surprise than the acceleration, caught for the first time off balance, Michel for a moment could think of nothing but to tighten the grip of his other hand, as hard as possible.

Dimly he sensed how both of their hydrogen lamps drew power, escalating forces with their stubborn masters' wills.

... not going to be beaten here by any little ...
... all right if you want to play REALLY ROUGH ...

Around the spinning pair of them the lunar mountains whirled. Down into the regolith their buffered bodies blurred, hurling slow waves of gravel, scythes of sand. Michel felt not a bit of fear; he was far too absorbed in other things, a hundred of them, mostly new, new doorways opening everywhere, new wonders thronging to discovery.

With one portion of his/Lancelot's mind he slowed down time by speeding up his own reactions, till now he could have plucked a millisecond out precisely from the endless spikefence of the marching past. Still, Frank's forcefield paw, the one that had slapped down the drone, had taken its enormous shape and was swinging at Michel almost before Michel could realize it. The man had drawn upon some hidden reserve of speed, his almost magical mental agility. This, thought Michel, is what has set him apart from other humans at ship controls, what has kept him alive in space against berserker after berserker. This something extra, at the last moment, at the end . . .

And before Michel's thought had been concluded, the sparring match was over.

". . . Marcus . . ."

". . . get some . . ."

". . . out there . . ."

". . . assistance . . ."

". . . boy back here . . ."

". . . one's down . . ."

Receding in a bounding flight across the rolling lunar surface, Frank's Lancelot flapped forcefields like ruined wings with the ferocious velocity of its spin. Skipping a small crater, glancing upward from a hillock, trailing disconnected alpha waves of thought, it spun toward the distant launching pad where white-garbed toys were scattering. Slow lunar gravity finally brought Frank crashing down again, amid a fresh spray of fine material from the surface. And now it dragged his tattered gauze-webs to a halt.

The watching winner, drifting a meter above the ground, poised still at the place where the fight had ended. Though he could not yet understand the ending of the fight, he could still feel it, in the thin muscles of his right shoulder.

Wondering, he began to drift a little higher. He did not fly to Frank; he could tell from the alpha waves of a stunned but living brain that Frank was still alive, inside that small, crumpled complex of force and metal upon which machines and human beings were now converging from all directions of the plain. But there would be little or nothing that he, Michel, could do in the way of giving help.

In the distance circled the sun-touched hills, looking more golden now than silver. Michel rose just a little higher still.

"Michel." There was a new strain in Tupelov's radio voice, and also a new fear starting. "Michel, come down."

He didn't much like Tupelov, despite the man's good manners; right from the start he hadn't liked him. There was no need to answer him right away. Frank was probably going to be all right, but now there would be no more testing for a while—maybe three days, Michel guessed. And before he took off the suit there was a thing or two he was impatient to get a look at.

Kid, you all right? This was Frank, half-conscious now, subvocalizing. *Kid, this is a tougher thing than any of us realized.*

"I understand Frank." He didn't bother, this time, to turn his radio off before he spoke. "Anyway I'm starting to."

"Michel, come down."

Come at me harder this time . . . I won't hurt you . . . The mumbled words cut off abruptly. Some of the medics and their robots had reached Frank already, assessed his condition, opened his dented ovoid, were administering medication that knocked him out completely.

Michel rose higher. Beyond the hills where sun-light had a grip would lie the rim of the full Earth.

"Michel!" Tupelov was in a swift agony of alarm. "Get down here! The defenses will pick you up; you're entering the danger zone . . ."

He knew all that. Without difficulty he could feel the vast electronic nerve-nets just beyond the near horizon, on all sides. The defense machines could not locate him yet, not really, but they were twitching with his presence. Ignorant gods, idiotic genius genii of metal and force.

He had to give them words to say to him: *Are you fast, little one in the gauze suit? Are you powerful? Will you play against berserkers, as we do? We dare you to a trial. Dare dare dare dare—*

Not ready for that, not yet, Michel turned away from the Earth, sank ten centimeters lower. As he turned his back on Earth the forcefields shielding his eyes went gold-opaque. In a moment his mind had cleared them enough to let him see Earth's risen god. There were great slow undulations of corona, and on the disc itself the flares and ulcerous sunspots. The solar wind came sleeting in his face, infinitesimally faint but he could see it if he tried.

Great things out there, that someone—like me—can somehow, sometime, begin to know. On even terms, maybe? Or do I only think that because of still-enormous ignorance?

"Michel?" The voice was still afraid, but now it was starting to be calculating as well.

No need to make Tupelov sweat so dangerously. Michel did not have to hurry, to do what must be done. More learning, first. More exploration of what was possible. And then?

"I'm coming," said Michel. In quiet obedience he coasted down to land.

FIVE

LOMBOK FOUND ELLY TEMESVAR IN AN ENORMOUS AND ancient city of old Earth, where the air was rich, untamed, with live-Earth smells, very different from those of all the other worlds Lombok had visited, very fitting, he thought, to the human senses. Temesvar's address was in a part of the city so old that it seemed half monument and maybe one-fourth archaeological site. The remainder in private hands included the great structure identified to Lombok as the Temple of the Final Savior. Its walls were granite block, aged steel reinforcements here and there showing through their fabric. Their style was some branch of Gothic. Just inside the doorway by which Lombok entered, a bright electroplaque informed the visitor of the different theories regarding the time and the purpose of the original construction—the place had been a temple of some kind, it seemed certain, from the very start.

An old-looking man with empty eyes, garbed in a gray sack, approached after Lombok had stood for an uncertain minute inside the arched dimness of the entry. When Lombok gave him the name of the woman he was looking for, he shuffled away again; Lombok continued waiting, looking mostly at the electroplaque.

A couple of minutes later, a blonde young woman of sturdy frame, veiled from the eyes down in well-fitting gray, emerged from behind a dull shimmer of modern field-drapes.

"You have a question for me?" Her voice was businesslike. It didn't seem to surprise her at all that a stranger should have a question.

"If you are Elly Temesvar, I have a question or two. *About* you, actually."

Above the veil, gray eyes appraised him levelly. "No reason why I shouldn't answer questions. Come along, we can talk in here."

He followed her past great columns, framing far interior spaces lost in dimness. Light from the gray Earth day outside entered through clerestory windows far above. Somewhere around a corner, a mixed chorus chanted drearily in a language Lombok did not recognize. He had been able to find out very little about this place as yet, and hadn't wanted to delay his visit until he could learn more. It was not on the secret Security list of possible goodlife front organizations—which of course proved nothing either way.

Elly led him across an enormous nave, whose immensity dwarfed small groups of gray-robes standing here and there in what looked like contemplation. At the far end of the nave rose what appeared to be a huge altar badly in need of repair. What with more pillars, and the pervading dimness, Lombok got no very clear look in that direction. Presently he was led into an out-of-the-way corner surrounded by still more columns, containing ancient stonework decorations and the first chairs Lombok had seen since entering the Temple. All the chairs looked old; some of them had once been real furniture, and some were cheap.

As his guide sat down, she simultaneously unveiled her face, saving her visitor the trouble of trying to frame a polite request along that line. Her appearance matched the photos Lombok had studied. "So, what are your questions, Mr.—?"

"Lombok. I'm from the Defense Department."

He had credentials ready, but Temesvar waved them away. "I believe you. Anyway, it doesn't matter."

Oh? Lombok wondered silently. Even if I were to ask you something about highly classified material? Of course whatever secrets the woman had known when on active duty would now be greatly out of date. Or most of them would.

Aloud he said, "I'm doing a psychological study on certain retired veterans. You filled out a census form last year, remember? We're just spot-checking some randomly chosen respondents."

"Randomly." For some reason, that amused her, or almost did. "If anything happens at random, it'll fall on me."

He almost looked up at her sharply, hearing that. Randomness related to certain official secrets she did know, secrets still kept in hiding on the Moon.

He was consulting a convincing-looking list. "Your resignation, let me see, was perfectly voluntary, wasn't it? No pressure put on you of any kind, for any reason?"

"There was a little pressure to change my mind, stay with the service, as I recall. I was really pretty good."

"Yes. You were." He paused. "Looking back at it now, what would you say was the real reason you resigned?"

"The same reason I gave then. I had begun to understand that what I was doing in the service did not matter."

Lombok gave her a chance to elaborate on that. When nothing came, he started making notes, painstakingly: "Did . . . not . . . matter."

"Aren't you recording this? Most people do."

Most people? How many interviewers had she had, and who were they? "If you don't mind—"

"Not in the least."

Lombok pretended to turn on a tiny recorder that had been running all along. "Now. Could you amplify that a little, about your career in the Space Force not mattering?"

"It just didn't. Military things don't, nor does exploring space. After my last mission I began to understand that. Not all at once, but gradually."

"The defense of the life of the galaxy against berserkers doesn't matter?"

"I knew you were going to put it that way. In the long run—no, it doesn't. Oh, we're not goodlife here in the Temple. If there were berserkers attacking Earth at this moment, I'd fight them, I suppose. Yes, I'm sure I would, a human reaction to protect the people that I'd see around me, and, I suppose, myself. Even though I knew that ultimately it wouldn't matter."

Lombok was trying to understand. "You just couldn't see that any more reconnaisance missions were worthwhile."

She was pleased, a little, that he was making an effort to grasp what she meant. "Something like that," she said.

"Want to tell me about that last mission of yours?"

She shifted position, crossing her legs athletically under the gray robing. "If you have the time to listen."

"All the time in the world." Lombok gestured genially. "Where you went, what you saw and did. How you got on with Colonel Marcus."

"Colonel, now, is he? Somehow I pictured him as having more rank than that by this time. Or being dead." It was said quite remotely, but without malice.

Lombok said, "I'm sure you've told the story of that last mission of yours before now."

"Yes, it's been recorded before, too. You could have looked it up. Probably you did. I admit I'm a little curious. Why do you come and ask me to tell it again, eleven years later?"

He didn't know whether or not to try and keep up the fiction of the random survey. "It was a unique experience. Wasn't it? I'd just like to hear it from you live, if you don't mind."

"Mind? No." But intelligent Elly was reevaluation him. She dug out smokers, offered one which Lombok refused, puffed her own into life. "Who do you work for, at Defense?"

"Tupelov."

She digested that for a moment, then gestured that it did not matter. "All right. Well, the big thing about that last mission of course was that we ran into something near the Core that we had never heard of, seen, or imagined before. It had been sighted at least once before, and photographed. But there are so many weird things in CORESEC they didn't even try to brief us on them all. Anyway. When we got back to CORESEC headquarters with—what we brought—people started calling the thing that we had found the Taj, after the Taj Mahal here on Earth. Something large and grand, with an aura of mystery about it.

That became its official code name. What you call it now I don't know."

"What did you think of the Taj? At first sight?"

Her eyes, which had begun to drift away from him, came back.

"At first of course it was just a place to go. A hope. You have to realize that our ship had been under attack almost continuously for almost twenty standard hours, by a berserker much more powerful than we were. No one but Frank Marcus could have ... anyway, by the time the Taj came into sight I was on the verge of a mental breakdown. I realize that now. They did hospitalize me briefly as soon as we got back to CORESEC headquarters, as you must know."

He knew. He signaled sympathetic, full attention. Elly looked at her smoker and put it out. "What I said a minute ago, about random things falling on me. Do you know that on that mission everything peculiar seemed to happen?"

"Such as what?"

"I'm not sure I can even recall the whole list of oddities now. Before the berserker jumped us, we found amino acids in free space, varieties that no one had every observed outside of atmosphere before. All kinds of organics, in enormous profusion."

"Excuse me, but I have never heard what the basic purpose of that mission was."

"General intelligence-gathering. Not looking for berserkers, certainly, not with two people in one small ship." The young woman fell silent, perhaps with some private memory.

"You were telling me about all the organic materials."

"Right. We were surprised. There are very few planets, you know, in that sector near the Core."

"CORESEC. I know a little bit about it. But tell me."

"High average star-density, better than thirty per cubic parsec. Nebular material very heavy, very complex. A maze of tunnels and bottlenecks; it's easy for a ship to get trapped. A number of them have. That's why they sent Frank."

"And you."

"Yes, I suppose. I was good. We saw gluts of petroleum. Would you believe dense enough in places for real gas-fires? Where there was free oxygen too, in regions sheltered from heavy starlight, you could get a line of real flame a billion kilometers long, along a zone of compression in the medium."

Another pause. Lombok got the feeling that when she had started to talk she had intended to lead up to something, but now she kept drifting away from it again. No doubt because nothing mattered. He prompted: "On that trip you became pregnant."

"Yes. I didn't realize you knew about that. I was on contraceptives, naturally. If I had wanted a pregnancy that wouldn't have been the ideal time or place to start it."

"Naturally."

"But for some reason there was a contraceptive failure. On that trip, all the long shots came home first."

It seemed that going on with the conversation was among the things that did not matter. Not wanting to concentrate too obviously on the pregnancy, he asked, "Tell me how you got away from the berserker."

Now Elly was looking past Lombok, as if at a viewscreen somewhere, and as she began to speak again tension gradually developed. Her strong hands started pulling and fingering at her robe.

"It was after us—I mean right after us, a few kilometers, no more. I think that by then it had decided it could take us easily, and it wanted us alive. As we entered the Taj, there was some kind of—shock, sudden change, don't ask me exactly what. Frank was knocked out. I remained conscious the whole time—at least when they hypnotized me back at CORESEC, they couldn't find any gaps in my consciousness."

"And what did you see, feel, experience, while you were in there?" There was no immediate answer, and Lombok added, "How long did this—immersion—last?"

The brief glance Elly gave him was almost pitying. "How long did it last? Well, the ship's clock in Frank's compartment ran through about four hours during the immersion, as you call it. The clock on my side meanwhile recorded something over eleven years."

Lombok had seen those figures before. He cleared his throat. "Obviously not any relativistic effect."

"Obviously." She smiled briefly. "Or I would have come out of the Taj with a half-grown child."

"So, some kind of strange field or whatever fouled up the timers. They were the regular cesium-133 clocks?"

"Yes. Therefore atoms of cesium-133 were changing energy states in our two compartments in quite different ways. If you were a scientist you'd look more puzzled than you do."

"Oh, I'm puzzled. But that's nothing new for me. Was your pregnancy affected by whatever had happened? Was the later fetal development normal?"

"I really don't know. There were other people willing to worry about that. And able to do a better job of taking care of it than I could, I'm sure.

I had all I could handle, for a while, inside my own head. I had the conceptus removed on Alpine, the first place we stopped. You know, this is the first time I've really talked about it since. It was a nice-looking adoption agency, as I recall, well-equipped ... I suppose there's an eleven-year-old running around Alpine now with a stranger origin than he or she can well imagine." Elly's expression softened, without quite reaching anything that could be called a smile.

Lombok sat back in his chair, raised his arms in a luxurious stretch. He looked up and around, at the dim groining of the ancient arches. "Who is the Final Savior, if you don't mind my asking?"

"I don't mind. We will know It when It comes."

"It?"

"When we say that, people tend to think we are berserker-worshippers. Completely untrue. The Savior is, will be, beyond the classifications of life and non-life."

"Identified with omnipotence? With a Creator?"

"I don't see any meaning in those questions."

Lombok cheerfully let them pass. "You were going to tell me more about your experience inside the Taj."

"Yes." Elly saw her hands plucking at the gray robe, and made them stop. "Descriptions won't do much good, I'm afraid. I tried to make recordings, take pictures. They didn't show very much when we got home."

"I know. If it hadn't been for the two things you brought back, it's possible no one would have believed your story at all."

There was a flash of humor in her eyes. "I didn't want to bring up the subject of those artifacts. Security, you know."

"I thought security wouldn't matter to you."

"It must matter to you, though. Now I'm sure

you are really from Defense. Tell me, have more
people been sent to the Taj? Oh, they must have
been, by this time. I'd like to know what they've
found out."

So would I, Lombok thought drily. Neither of
the two expeditions had returned as yet. Which
was not necessarily a sign of anything really
wrong, not yet, but certainly in another standard
year it would begin to be. He said, "I'm not really
in the exploration end of the business."

Elly was once more looking over his shoulder.
"You want to hear what it was like. All right. At
one point, for example, it was as if—as if the ship
had been turned inside out, and shrunken to the
size of a giant beach-ball. Spherical still, but
hardly bigger than a human body. I sat there
somehow, on this intricate thing, riding—like a
sort of side-saddle. My own body—I couldn't tell
if my body was inside out too, or not. I'm sure I
wasn't dreaming. My head was giant-sized and
stuck out unprotected."

"Didn't you have your suit on?"

"Yes. When the experience started. But then I
seemed to be outside of it."

"Colonel Marcus was unconscious all this
time?"

"Yes. Commander Marcus, then. I couldn't raise
him on the intercom, which had changed into the
weirdest little squiggle of wire. I looked around
the—the beach-ball, but I couldn't identify anything belonging to the ship."

"And what about things outside the ship? Away
from it?"

There was a longer pause than any yet. Elly
might have been working out a complex math
problem in her mind.

"Order," she answered at last. "And disorder,
too. But maybe what looked like, felt like chaos

was only order, arrangement, of a higher kind than I could understand."

"Can't you tell me anything more concrete?"

"I can. But I don't think it'll help you in grasping the total experience." She gave a sharp sigh, started again. "When you're dreaming, the concept or feeling comes into your mind first, and then the brain generates pictures as an appropriate accompaniment. This wasn't dreaming, definitely. But I think it worked in a similar way. First I was aware of order, and then I saw these great structural members surrounding our ship. Somehow I was able to appreciate, visualize, the distance scale. As if we were inside something like a geodesic dome, but bigger than a star. I've never had an experience like that before. I don't suppose I ever will again.

"I was aware of disorder, or apparent disorder, things going on that made no sense at all to me. And with that I visualized a mist, more like a water-droplet fog than nebula, so thick that I could see it whipping past, right beside the ship. And there were sounds—I can't really recall them, let alone describe them. But they affected me in the same way. Order and disorder alternating. Music, but not like—and I had the feeling that if I could have stopped the ship, I could have joyfully spent my life in trying to unravel the mysteries in just one handful of that fog rushing past. . . ."

Elly's hands were still now, but white-knuckled. Her face was almost serene, but Lombok to his astonishment thought he saw the beginnings of tears in those far-looking eyes.

For some reason this depth of feeling in her made him a little nervous, a little embarrassed, almost a little angry. "At debriefing," he said, "you didn't report—an experience of that intensity."

Her gaze came back to him. "I was numb," she

said, relaxing a trifle. "My feelings . . . have been growing, developing, ever since it happened."

Lombok was not satisfied. He said, "This thing, the Taj—it was only a couple of hours away, at sublight speeds, from at least one quite massive star. I mean the star emitting that plasma jet, in which you were trying to hide your ship."

"Yes."

"Well, doesn't that present a seeming inconsistency? Doesn't it suggest perhaps that this thing that made such an impression on you had no physical reality?" Lombok was not much impressed by mystical experiences; not when some people could attain them by inhaling the smoke of burning weeds.

"Yes, it does," Elly answered calmly. "Or it would, rather, if I thought the Taj was just a physical construct of stellar size. Then tidal factors and other things would seem to make that kind of close proximity impossible. But I can only report things as they were."

"Or as they seemed to you."

"You yourself mentioned the two things we brought back. Proof of some kind of unusual encounter, certainly."

"Certainly." He had some theories of his own about them, but now was not the time. He was letting himself be distracted from what he had come here for. "Sorry I interrupted; go on. You went into the Taj, and the berserker came in after you, presumably."

"I saw it inside, following us, for a while. Wait. First, it—it said something, on voice radio, about how our new weapons weren't going to help us. Then we went in, and it came in, following us . . . and then . . . I don't know. It was destroyed, perhaps. Or it lost us. Or it just—gave up."

"Gave up? How could a berserker—?"

"I don't know. I . . . the funny thing is, once we were inside, I think I all but forgot about the berserker."

"You were piloting the whole time you were inside?"

"I took the controls, on manual, when Frank conked out. Then somewhere along the line we went on autopilot, because I do remember clearly, after we had emerged again, switching the autopilot off and taking back manual control."

"You were back in normal space then?"

"What passes for normal, in CORESEC. And Frank was coming round, and by then the Taj was out of sight. As soon as Frank started to get on top of the situation again, he made some little joke about how he'd rested. When I tried to tell him what had happened, he thought I was, or had been, delirious. *Then* we found the two artifacts, the astragalus in his cabin, the ring in mine. They were just sitting on our consoles, right out in the open. We picked them up—didn't know what to make of them. It wasn't until later, at CORESEC base, that their—properties—were discovered."

"Yes." Lombok pondered for a while. "Did Frank ever know that you were pregnant?"

Elly didn't spend much time thinking about it. "I really don't know, he never said anything. He's had other children here and there; now and then he'd mention the fact in passing, as you might mention having had your appendix out. Don't tell me he's expressing a personal interest now."

"Not that I know of." Here came a few tourists, or prospective converts maybe, crossing the nave behind a gray-robed guide. The tourist man carried a rather weighty single-handled case which probably meant he was going to make some elaborate holographs.

Elly was lighting herself another smoker. "Something's come up, though, hasn't it?" she insisted. "Having to do with the kid."

Lombok appeared to take thought. "He'd be about ten now, wouldn't he? Are you developing a personal interest of your own?"

"Eleven. You said 'he.' "

"You didn't ask them about the sex at the adoption agency, when you—?"

There was a step behind Lombok, and he turned to see one of the tourist women bending close. Why should she want to ask him a question, when she had a guide? But it wasn't a question anyway, because the woman had something in her hand, and there was a new coolness in Lombok's face and lungs.

Stupid joke, he thought, and started to get up, and knew that he was falling down instead.

SIX

"HEY, MICHEL, THAT WAS ONE LOVELY COUNTER-punch." In the low-ceilinged, hard-surfaced Moon-base corridor the voice issuing from Frank's speakers took on a small tail of ringing echo, and if Michel had been wearing Lancelot he might have found some amusement in trying to sort out the several sets of what he had learned were called harmonics. But he was in his loafing clothes to-day, shorts and loose shirt and sandals, taking a lone and moody stroll that had led him farther and farther from the busier regions of the base. He hadn't seen anyone at all for a couple of min-utes before he came upon Frank's boxes standing motionless against a wall.

But Michel was at once glad of the meeting. "Thanks," he said. "I didn't mean to knock you out."

"I know. It's all right. No tests for you today?"

Two standard days had gone by since their sparring match. "Not today. Tomorrow I think we start again."

"*You* start again. They've informed me I won't have to wear the damned thing any more. What's up? You look a little worried."

"Well." There were really two things, neither of which he had yet mentioned to anyone else, not even to his mother. "For one thing, they're changing the equipment. Trying to fit extra weapons onto it. But—" Michel, almost despairing of trying to make his feelings on the subject convincing to anyone else, shook his head.

"You don't know if you can work the weapons properly."

"That's not it! Probably I can. But—the thing is, Lancelot really doesn't need them."

Frank moved a few centimeters from the wall, all segments rolling together. His voice sounded alarmed and hardly mechanical at all. "Hey, kid. Eventually, you know, whoever wears that thing is supposed to fight berserkers with it."

"I know."

"That was a good pillow-fight that you and I had, but as a test it was very preliminary. If that had been a berserker machine instead of me ... nobody's going to punch one of those things out with his fist."

"I know! I mean, I know what you mean, Frank. But—I think I could. With Lancelot. Once I really learn how Lancelot works."

Michel could almost see Frank's head shaking inside its box. "Kid. Michel. Look. Maybe it is theoretically possible for Lancelot to draw that kind of power. But the enemy uses the same power sources we do, roughly speaking. And Lancelot right now doesn't have the hardware."

"You mean metal."

Frank had fallen silent. Michel, looking back

over his shoulder in the direction he himself had come from, saw the dark-skinned woman from the scientific group, approaching at a graceful walk. Not in her spacesuit now of course, but wearing a dress whose draped skirt somehow, with her moving in it, suggested tall grass and elegantly drooping trees moved by a light wind.

"Michel," said Frank's speakers in a tone that was subtly new, "this is Vera. Mrs. Tupelov."

"Hello," said Michel, and, as Mother would have expected, made a polite greeting gesture.

The woman's heavy lips were not pouty at all when she was smiling. "I know Michel, everyone does. Call me Vera, will you, honey?"

Still, a certain strain was in the air. Some awkwardness having to do with the way adults conducted their social lives had just happened, or was happening right now. Into the silence Frank said, "Michel and I were just talking about Lancelot. The difficulties thereof."

"Oh?" Vera looked properly concerned. "If it's not about the forcefield math, I'm afraid I can't help much."

"More like piloting problems," Michel said unhappily.

"Honey, if it's getting to you after all, you better tell the medics." Vera's concern grew more real. "Or tell my husband. Or I'll tell him for you."

"Getting to me? Oh no. It's not that I get sick using Lancelot, or anything like that."

Frank's middle box put out two metal stick-arms, let them swing rhythmically from their upper joints. It seemed to be a gesture miming patience, taking the place perhaps of slow thumb-twiddling.

Vera saw this and shook her head. "Look, boys, I think I'll just leave you to your piloting discussion. Catch you later, both of you."

"Caaatch yoouu." Frank's answer came in a voice for once tuned far outside the human vocal spectrum, deep as the cough of some giant predator.

Vera giggled. With a wink in Michel's direction and a small wave for both of them she turned in her swinging skirt and strode back in the way that she had come, leaving Michel with a momentary vague curiosity as to why she had come this way at all.

But he had more demanding things to think about. "Can I ask you something, Frank?"

"Sure. If I can ask you something, too."

"What?"

"Promise you'll try to teach me how you do it. With Lancelot. When there's time."

Michel paused. "I'll try."

"You don't sound too hopeful. Anyway, what was your question?"

Michel drew a deep breath, and with the sensation of stepping into a gulf of unknown depth he asked, "Do you ever have the feeling that you're becoming some kind of a machine?"

"Is that all? Hell, no. Well of course in a sense this hardware that you see has become a part of me. But *I'm* not a part of anything except myself . . . oh, maybe you mean when piloting a ship? Yeah, then there's a sense, a very strong sense sometimes, in which the ship and pilot become a unit. But I had that feeling, pretty much the same, before I was all smashed up. It's a pilot's feeling of becoming more than he is otherwise."

"Not of being swallowed up by anything, though."

"Swallowed up? No." Frank paused, his liquid lenses sliding and rotating carefully. "That answer your question?"

"I don't know. No it doesn't, really."

"Ah. To me, Lancelot doesn't feel like a machine at all. If it was a machine, felt like a machine, then I could live with it. But to you it does, and the machine part is taking over the live part, is that it? The live part being you?"

"Yes." It was a surprising relief to have said that much, at last, to someone.

"This feeling ends, I trust, when you take the damned thing off."

"Yeah. Only . . ."

"Why don't you complain about it, as Vera suggested?"

"Then they might not let me wear it." Confession, coming almost in a whisper. "I feel happier when I have it on. And then like there's less of me, or something, every time when they take me out of it again."

"Hell." A heartily sympathetic though mechanized snort. "*I'm* happier when I'm in a ship."

That wasn't it, though. Or was it? Michel didn't feel sure enough to argue. And certainly he felt better for confession. Even—or especially—to a set of boxes.

Frank remained silent for more than five seconds, which was for him a long and thoughtful pause. "Let's take a walk," his speakers grunted then.

Michel caught up with a skip to the swiftly moving train, and then walked quickly to hold his place beside it. He was led purposefully back into the regions where other people and other moving machines were common.

A liquid lens on the head box was studying Michel. Frank asked, "I don't suppose they've shown you any of the pseudopersonalities."

"The what? No."

"I don't know why in hell he doesn't communicate with you. It would give you a better perspective on the whole operation."

They passed signs warning about security zones. They passed one live guard, for whom Frank did not even slow.

"Colonel Marcus? I should see the kid's clearance, if he's going—"

"Stuff it. *You* should have a clearance, just to talk to *him*."

That behind them, they kept walking and rolling on. Then Frank stopped abruptly, before a plain door with no handle. He put out one of his metal arms and with a touch on the door's featureless surface transmitted some kind of opening code. It opened to let them enter a small and heavily shielded storeroom.

There were a couple of narrow aisles, between low racks. Each rack held hundreds of metal cases, each case being of a size for an adult to carry about one-handed, and fitted with an appropriate grip.

Frank rolled between the racks, inspecting labels. "These are the little bastards we're supposed to replace in the Lancelot system. Or rather you, and other kids like you if they ever find any, are going to replace 'em. *I* can't hack it. I really can't."

"I don't understand." The cases held complex components of some kind, meant to be plugged into something larger. Beyond that Michel could get no feeling for them.

With a metal arm Frank drew a case down from a rack. Then he trundled down the aisle with it to the end of the room, where work space had been provided, and slid it expertly into a large console. He made adjustments on a viewer, and a moment later beckoned to Michel.

Looking in, through what seemed to be some great power of optical magnification, Michel could see what at first glance appeared to be imitation snowflakes, cobbled together out of what might be plastic, in a complex and vast array.

Frank's voice beside him said, "This one's the *Red Baron*. Quite a story connected with it. Some of the others here have seen use in combat too, incorporated into conventional fighting ships as well as earlier versions of Lancelot. In places where live human brains tend to fail under the strain. These stand the strain, but they can't really do the job. Not well enough."

The name *Red Baron* meant nothing to Michel, who was discovering how to tune the viewer. His adjustments led him down through level after level of magnification. When light-quanta became too coarse to image the next level of detail properly, electrons were automatically substituted, and quarkbeams succeeded those grosser entities in turn. The crystalline complexity that had suggested snowflakes was still present, composed of what form of matter Michel could no longer guess, diminishing apparently without limit into finer and finer delicacies.

"This looks like—like something natural. But it isn't."

"Nope. People made it. Go on, tune it finer if you like."

He did, until the device reached its ultimate limit. The interior of the pseudopersonality was like no other artifact that Michel had ever examined. The smaller the scale on which he looked at it, the finer and more perfect its structure appeared.

"These are imitation personalities, kid, most of them modeled on historical individuals. Imitation minds, of a sort. They were invented to be used in historical simulations, and in desperation the powers who run things have tried to make 'em work in space combat. Instead of the subconscious minds of living brains. There are parts of our minds that live outside of time, you know."

"I've heard that. I don't know if it's—"

"It's true. It's what gives us the edge, sometimes, over the enemy. One of the things that does."

Michel was not listening very carefully. He was awed by what he saw—not by the thing's capabilities so much as by its workmanship, which impressed him even more than Lancelot's. He murmured something.

"They work in fractal dimensions when they make these, Michel. Know what that means?"

Michel shrugged. He didn't expect to comprehend the specialized words that adult technologists used among themselves. "Something very small, I guess."

"It's roughly like this: A line has one dimension, a point has none. Fractal involves something in between."

Michel raised his eyes from the viewer, prodded the pseudopersonality's case with one finger where it partially projected from the console. "And this can replace a human operator in Lancelot?"

"Not very well, as I say, or we wouldn't be here. Anyway, you better believe they wouldn't put this particular pseudo in."

"Why not?"

"It has to do with who the real Red Baron was. Someone they wouldn't want to trust with Lancelot. Like me." Frank's speakers emitted a series of rising squeals that Michel understood as sardonically formalized laughter. "But hell, even I can outdo these in Lancelot. Which is the point I wanted to make when I brought you here. You and I are alive, and this stuff is hardware. Some people around here who talk a lot of philosophical crap have trouble with that distinction." Contempt had grown in Frank's voice. "If these things, the finest machines we can make, could do my job better than I can, Tupelov wouldn't have dragged you all the way here from Alpine, and we wouldn't be taking you out to the proving grounds in a couple more days. We're human beings. We're the bosses when it comes to any partnership with machines. And also we're gonna win the war. If anyone should ask you."

"Frank? Two more questions?"

"Shoot."

"Who's really going to be using Lancelot in combat?"

A five-second hesitation. "Someone who can use it really well."

Michel nodded slowly; it was an answer he had, really, already known. And it was something that he was going to have to think about. "Second question. Where are the proving grounds?"

"Christ, they don't tell you anything. The moons and the rings of Uranus make up the one we're going to use. It takes about six hours to get out there from here."

SEVEN

EVEN BEFORE ELLY TEMESVAR WAS FULLY AWAKE, HER body and mind had at some level recognized the subtle differences between natural gravity at the Earth's surface and artificial gravity set at a level of not quite one standard G. She had been dreaming of mountains, and a log building with a peaked roof . . .

So when her eyes opened it was with more curiosity than surprise that she discovered herself to be lying on her back on a berth in a small cabin. Her surroundings did not much resemble the interior of any service ship that she had ever ridden in, being decorated in an ornate and obviously civilian style, and her curiosity increased.

In the next moment, memory returned with a rush. An immediate attempt to jump to her feet got her nowhere at all; something was holding her almost motionless. Straining her neck somewhat, she could just manage to raise her head enough

to look down at her body. Over her gray Temple
garments ran some kind of webbing, laced to the
frame of the berth at many points. Her mind,
seeking frantically for reassurance, could come up
with nothing better than the feeble suggestion that
the bonds might be meant only as an emergency
restraint against strong acceleration. But in that
case there ought to be some way for the occupant
to loose the bindings, and she could discover none.
She could move little more than her fingertips.

. . . As she now recalled the scene, she had simply taken them for tourists. Tourists were coming
and going in the Temple at all hours, frequently,
and there had seemed to be no reason for her to
inspect this small group closely. Elly closed her
eyes now, trying to remember. Two women and a
man, the man white-haired she thought, following
Deacon Mabuchi across the nave, approaching the
place where Elly sat talking with her visitor. Now
she could summon up a vague recollection of
something rather small but evidently heavy, carried swinging in the man's left hand. The group
had proceeded casually right up to where she sat
with Lombok, and then . . . then it had been too
late. Now she remembered seeing Lombok go
down, just before she had blacked out herself. So
it would seem that Lombok had not been a willing
partner in her kidnapping, or whatever this might
be.

Across the tiny cabin, almost within arm's reach
had she been able to reach out an arm, there was
another berth. But it was unoccupied, folded back
to make part of the bulkhead.

A moment later, a door near Elly's head slid
open. A tall, white-haired man in silvery civilian
clothing looked in at her calmly from a narrow
corridor outside. "Are you at all hurt?" he asked,

sounding mildly concerned, and also very much in control.

At second glance, Elly judged that her visitor's hair was not age-white but only extremely blond, as if he were a natural albino who had elected to have repigmentation treatment limited to his eyes, which were a very pale blue, and his skin, of an untanned Caucasian pallor. He was waiting for an answer.

Elly moved her fingers, about all that she could do in the way of testing. "I don't think so," she answered, trying to sound calm.

"We had to act abruptly. We could not take the risks of argument." It was not an apology, only an explanation. "But I hope to be able to release you soon, Ms. Temesvar."

"What keeps you from releasing me now? And who are you?"

"You can call me Stal. It means 'steel,' in an old language, and I rather like it." He spoke as if his likes and dislikes were important things indeed. Elly realized that to his helpless prisoner they might well prove to be important.

Stal continued: "You really are among friends aboard this ship." The words seemed meant as reassurance, but his set features did not soften at all as he spoke. He glanced out into the corridor behind him now, and made a small beckoning motion with his head. A moment later he pressed himself back against the bulkhead, making room in the narrow doorway for a figure familiar to Elly, that of a stocky man of middle height, with Oriental features and black hair. This was Deacon Mabuchi, like Elly still wearing Temple gray, a soft smock above work trousers and plain boots.

The Deacon stood beside her berth, his round face glowing down at her with some triumph she could not comprehend. He murmured gently, "Sister Temesvar—"

"Deacon, explain to me—"

The Deacon mildly overrode her protest. "All now aboard this ship, Sister Temesvar, are in fact our fellow Heralds of the Savior, though they do not yet admit it, even to themselves. The fact is that the Savior has come, and these folk, unlike our own titular leaders in the Temple, have recognized It."

Elly didn't know what to say. For her, allegiance to the Temple faith had been only the path of least resistance, acceptable as truth because every other belief or mental attitude seemed to have been blocked, made practically impossible by what she had witnessed and experienced at the Core.

Mabuchi's own faith was obviously something quite different. While Stal stood back, watching the two of them as imperturbably as before, the Deacon's eyes shone down exultantly, possessively, at Elly.

"And you, Sister Temesvar, you are the most fortunate of women. Today, the only glory that can matter has become yours. It is through you that the Savior has taken final form for us. Through you life and death alike will be no more. Through you the Earth and all that has grown from Earth will attain final peace."

There was a silence in the small cabin. Three people, each one looking from one face to the other of the remaining two, expectantly. Each one, thought Elly, with a purpose at right angles to the other two, so none of them really understood another.

Her own purpose right now was simply to get free. "All this has some connection with my child, doesn't it?" she demanded sharply. Getting free meant arguing with these men, and arguing would seem to require knowing what they wanted and expected. And Lombok had been digging for information on the subject of her offspring. Something *had* come up. . . .

"Child no longer," intoned Mabuchi. The words that began pouring from him now sounded like a quotation from some secret ritual that Elly had never heard before: "Flesh of man and woman no longer, though still in a fleshly garment robed . . ."

Stal chimed in: "Lord of force and metal, Lord free of life and death alike . . ." It was impossible to tell if his harsh voice held mockery or struggled to restrain true feeling. Watching Stal, Elly was suddenly struck with the idea that the man looked the way he did because of a deliberate attempt to cultivate a metallic appearance. This idea in turn suggested something else to her, something that made her abruptly begin to feel faint. Stop that, she ordered herself.

And made herself interrupt the chanting men: "Where are you taking me, and why?"

Mabuchi deferred to Stal, and it was the white-haired man who answered: "We are taking you to meet the entity who was your son, Ms. Temesvar. That means going out to the new military proving grounds, out in the Uranian system."

That was an answer that explained nothing, that in fact seemed to make no sense at all. "Why should he be there?" Before leaving the service Elly had heard of the new proving grounds, but she had no idea of what might be going on there now.

"He is there because the badlife seek to use him." The epithet was frightening enough to bring on a new surge of faintness, all the more frightening because it slipped from Stal's lips with such unselfconscious ease. At the moment Elly could not remember ever hearing anyone use the word in real life before. It was a word from fiction, from the stage, on which the actors who played goodlife tended to emphasize it, striving for maximum shock effect.

Mabuchi too was moved, though for another reason. "The Savior should not be called 'he,' " he protested to his colleague.

"I beg your pardon," the tall man responded stiffly. "But to this woman, the Savior is still her child. And we must try to attune ourselves to her psychology. —Ms. Temesvar, the badlife have grasped at least the fact that your offspring is unusual, and they mean to use him as part of a weapons system. Have you ever heard the code name *Lancelot*?"

"No," she answered weakly. Of course there were innumerable code names that she had never heard. She was trying to imagine what kind of weapons system might have her eleven-year-old plugged into it. Frank's child too, of course, and she could well imagine a boy of unusual ability. The whole idea still seemed insane to her, which did not mean that desperate men and women, Frank Marcus one of their number, were not going to come up with something like it for their next effort in the war. Elly's imagination presented her a picture of her child, amputated somehow to fit a set of Frank-like boxes, and fired off into the void. . . .

"From what we know of Lancelot it is a horror," Stal was saying. "And we intend to save Michel from it. Michel, that is what his adoptive parents named him. Here, Elly, I have a picture."

Metal-steady in Stal's wiry fingers, there appeared a photograph that had been taken somewhere out of doors. On a second-story porch on the front of a log building, a young boy stood gazing upward toward the camera. His hands, large and square-looking like a workman's, were on the railing and he squinted into a wind that pulled at his long, fair hair. Above his head the roof was steep and Elly, thinking *Alpine*, knew a chill of beginning conviction.

The clarity of the boy's face had been somehow enhanced, at the expense of peripheral details. He was good-looking, Elly thought, in a rather sharp-featured way, and in his forehead and in his eyes she involuntarily discovered something of herself. What there might be of Frank Marcus was not so easy to discover.

Both men were obviously waiting for her reaction. "Michel what?" she finally asked them.

"Geulincx," said Stal. "An eminent Alpine family you may have heard of. Folk art. Woodcarving."

"I haven't been paying much attention to art of any kind." At last she had produced a sentiment for which Mabuchi's face could register approval. "I still don't understand—except that you must think this kid is the Savior. And you think I am his mother. If so, is this the way you honor me?"

The men exchanged glances, after which Mabuchi went out, evidently controlling struggling emotions with a great effort.

"I expect you will be of great help to us," Stal explained then. "When we have Michel on board here, and when both you and he have truly grasped the situation. What happens when we liberate him from the badlife may very well be traumatic. Therefore—Savior or not—a mother's care may be important."

"You expect to simply land this ship at the proving grounds somewhere and load him on board, assuming he's really there? Without—"

"Without resistance from the badlife? No, lady,

I do not expect that. But provisions have been made." His stiff lips moved a trifle, almost smiling.

"Are you the captain of this ship, Stal?"

"I? No."

"I demand to see the captain, then."

"Your chance will come."

"Now."

"I have no orders to arrange such a meeting. But perhaps in this case I should use initiative." After staring at Elly a thoughtful moment longer, Stal suddenly bent and reached under her berth. His hand emerged holding a heavy metal case, and she was reminded at once of the thing she remembered seeing him carry in the Temple. There, to the degree that she had thought of it at all, she must have assumed that it was some kind of holography equipment, a common piece of tourist baggage.

Stal swung the empty berth opposite down from the wall. Then, with the care of one handling a valued object, he hoisted the case up into the berth, securing it there deftly with the common acceleration restraints. Then there was a click, as Stal opened a small door on the front of the case— or perhaps the door had opened automatically, Elly was not sure. Something very thin and snakily metallic drew itself out of the case, almost like a line sketched in the air. It reached across the space between berths for one of Elly's almost immobilized fingers, and stung her briefly.

"What—?"

The sinuous limb withdrew. Then, just above the place where the arm had disappeared, a new opening in the case revealed what looked like the subtle vibration of a broad-spectrum liquid lens. Elly had the uncomfortable impression that her whole form was being scanned intently.

"Just a little blood test, I should imagine," Stal said, in a voice that was possibly intended to be soothing. "The Co-ordinator will wish to make absolutely sure that you are who we think you are. And perhaps to confirm some details of Michel's genetic inheritance."

"You—imagine?" Elly had never before seen a robot medic that looked very much like—

From the small case issued words. They came in a ridiculously squeaky voice, which under other circumstances might possibly have offered her at least momentary amusement. The voice said sharply: "You will tell this life-unit nothing more without further orders."

Stal bowed at once. Stammering, he made humble acknowledgement of the Co-ordinator's command. But Elly could no longer see or hear him.

EIGHT

SOME TEN STANDARD YEARS AGO, OPERATIONS HEAD-
quarters for the new proving grounds had been
established on the surface of the Uranian satellite
Miranda. Under one dome the structure offered
room for a hundred humans to work and live;
some of the quarters could be called luxurious,
and all were at least reasonably comfortable. At
the order of the President of Earth provision had
also been made for housing members of any of the
very few known non-Earthly intelligent races. So
far none of these had ever appeared as guests.

"Told 'em when they built it that we'd never see
a Carmpan here." This from Tupelov, who today
was conducting a grand tour of the facility for one
lone and probably lonely guest. Walking normally
in the augmented gravity, he led Carmen Geulincx
from the lobby of the living quarters out into the
central operations room. Here one tall wall was

made up almost entirely of viewing ports, all of them at the moment cleared.

"Oh!" said Carmen. Then she added, quite unnecessarily, "That's Uranus itself."

The solar system of her homeworld contained no sight at all like this. Her hand on Tupelov's arm, they walked right up to the ports. The blue-green gas giant, a great scimitar of its surface in direct sunlight at the moment, seemed to be almost leaning right against the outer surface of the heavy glass. What could be seen of Miranda's own slaggy skin, just underneath and outside the port, was bathed by reflection from the planet, producing an eerie underwater glow.

Carmen hung back for a moment, and the Secretary tugged his arm forward, so that she came with him rather than let go. Standing just inside a port, he pointed out to her the moons Oberon and Ariel, each turning toward the distant Sun a bright miniature of Uranus' own crescent. The satellites were moving perceptibly, in the plane of the monster's spinbulging equator, and the same aquamarine light that lay on the Mirandan landscape tinged also the dull, scarred flanks that the two other visible moons turned toward their primary.

"Titania and Umbriel are evidently hiding behind Daddy at the moment," said Tupelov.

"And the rings . . ." breathed Carmen. "Ahh, beautiful."

"Sometimes you can't see them at all, even from here." But sometimes, as now, the great circlets, like ghosts of the rings of Saturn, worked like giant diffraction gratings, shredding cold sunlight into a nebulous multicolored spectrum, and sending a sample of it in through the ports. Tupelov tried a new metaphor: "A rainbow ballet skirt for a fat, dancing planet."

Carmen, perhaps through kindness, made no comment on that effort. "Where's Earth?" she asked at last.

He had to get right up against the glass and squint into the incoming Sunlight. "There. The bluish star." Carmen moved up close beside him and it felt natural to rest a pointing forearm on her shoulder; she was as tall as he.

"It looks so near Sol," she said tritely. Even at this altitude in the System there was no doubt which star lay at its center.

"It is. Very near. Out here we're nineteen times as far away. That's Mars, see, looking red, right beside the Earth."

"Yes. And I think I can recognize Venus now. Inward, looking brighter."

"Right you are."

"And beyond. That's Orion, isn't it?—you pointed it out to me from Moonbase. It doesn't look any different at all."

To Tupelov it looked bigger. They had left a village and climbed a little hill, and now looking back past the village they saw a distant mountain practically unchanged. In angular measurement a little shrunken, but in subjective vision magnified, because of the vast shrinkage of the houses and the streets that they had left behind.

For a human mind connected to Lancelot's well-nigh supernatural vision—what would the effect be like?

Tupelov asked, "How does Michel like all this traveling?"

"Oh, I think he enjoys it. Not that he ever tells me a lot about how he feels. Do you and Vera have any children, Mr. Tupelov?"

"No." He tried to make it sound just a bit regretful.

"You're very kind to take the time to show me all these things."

"Oh, not at all." It was time he would have had to use on things of secondary importance anyway, while Michel and the latest refinement of the equipment were being melded for the first tests at the proving grounds. "I'll tell you a secret," Tupelov continued, sounding confidential though there were twenty other people in the big room. "Being nice to certain people is part of my job, just as being nasty to others is part of it also. But for you I'd be nice anyway."

The athletic lady from far away didn't know quite what to make of that. Well, it seemed he didn't yet know his own mind regarding her, which was doubtless why he talked that way.

Turning away from the ports at last, he led her closer to the center of the room. "Here's the Moonbase ticker."

"Ticker? Why do you call it that?"

"I guess some of the ancient models actually used to tick. The name, as applied to remote printers, goes way back." Coming through as usual across the ticker's screens and on its writer were streams of information all more or less relevant to Defense. Some of the data were answers to questions transmitted from here down to Moonbase hours ago, and some were questions that the people down there had thought up for the Secretary or his aids during the few hours since he had left them. "See, when it takes more than two hours to beam a message one way, you don't wait for an answer, you just keep chattering." Tupelov briskly tapped the human operator's shoulder, and in a different tone demanded, "Any word from Lombok yet?"

"Negative, sir."

"Earth is *that* far." Carmen was musing aloud,

looking back toward the ports. "And that's two hours' communication time. And Alpine is *months* away, even moving at multiples of the speed of light. We can't really grasp it, can we? I can't anyway."

He was wondering whether he ought to try to commiserate with Carmen over her separation from her husband, when a double door opened on the far side of the big room. "Here we go," he said instead. "Here comes Michel."

The kid was garbed in Lancelot over a tight-fitting orange undersuit. As usual, he looked calm, intent, and ready to go. Carmen immediately hurried over to her son to make a little fuss about him, her hands stroking the invisible forcefields that guarded his face and tender neck as if there might be a collar there to be turned up. Then, with a technique she had discovered on Moonbase, she reached inside and actually touched his cheek. It could be done, as long as the reaching hand moved slowly enough, and the wearer was willing to be touched. Tupelov found himself wishing, not for the first time, that the damned thing *looked* more formidable; small wonder that half the brass were unable to generate any faith in it. It was much too late now, of course, to make any design changes for appearance's sake. But it would have been easier to sell to everyone if it had looked more like a suit of armor. Somehow this version didn't appear to be able to keep its wearer dry in the rain, let alone . . . Actually, it made the kid look like some kind of fairy in the school play.

Carmen, abruptly realizing that everyone else was waiting for her to get out of the way, dropped her hands and with a few nervous words took herself aside.

Tupelov stepped forward. "Michel, I hope this time you've been adequately briefed on what's expected. I hear we've been a little lax about that in the past."

Michel answered clearly. "They said that this time you just want me to fly all the way around Miranda."

"That's right. After you've done that we'll talk about what comes next. Some of us are going to be following along close beside you, in a scoutship. Ready?"

Elly Temesvar, recovering from her faint, had no idea how much time had elapsed since her introduction to the Co-ordinator, except that her body in its prolonged bondage was beginning to be uncomfortable in several ways. The restraints were as tight as ever. The door to the corridor was closed again, and the berth opposite hers had been swung back up into the bulkhead. She was alone.

Except, of course, that *it* might have ordered itself put back under the berth she lay upon.

It was time for a little deliberate deep breathing. She was not going to allow herself to sail off into another faint, no matter what. But fear and confinement were making her arms and legs feel so weak that she was not sure she would be able to stand up even if she were set free. . . .

The reopening of the cabin door actually came as a relief. A youngish, heavy-bodied woman looked in. Her heavy breasts seemed to be bound, to flatten them, by some constricting fabric underneath a steel-colored shirt. Elly could not tell if she was one more of the pseudo-tourists from the Temple or not.

"Where—" Elly began, and discovered that her mouth was now so dry that the simplest speech was difficult.

"Where what?" The woman's voice was harsh, like a reedy imitation of Stal's. She came to stand right beside the bunk, evidently with no fear in her legs of anything that might be beneath it. "Never mind. There's nothing that you need to know just yet."

"Get me a drink," Elly managed, in a whisper.

"All right. But don't make any fuss that's going to bother them out in the control room." What was probably the same spray device that had been used in the Temple appeared in the woman's hand. "Or off you go to sleep again."

Just as at Moonbase, a rink-sized portion of the Mirandan surface had been smoothed and prepared, and starting marks laid out. The natural gravity here was ridiculously weak, so that Michel-Lancelot drifted without even trying, and his suited human escorts were variously anchored and attached to one another with lines. For a small distance beyond the edges of the smoothed arena the floodlights made the natural land look like broken glass and cinders. The surface notched up frequently in man-sized sawteeth, local features nicking a dark horizon that circled the floodlit area and the adjacent operations building at a distance of no more than a few hundred meters. Uranus' polar cap of sunlight, half below the horizon now, still washed the landscape, the dark building and its docked scoutships, with fading underwater light.

In the opposite direction, the large moon that they had told Michel was called Oberon was shifting his own tiny crescent, as swifter Miranda in her smaller orbit began to overtake him. When Michel had first heard the names, he had wondered briefly about coincidence; but right now there were other things that seemed to need wondering about more.

From here, Lancelot's eyes could scan interplanetary space with fair efficiency, in particular the regular approach lanes leading to the solar system's inner harbors. Without much effort Michel could pick out a least a dozen spaceships of various sizes, moving in their several directions at various speeds. Though all of the ships that he could see looked spherical, and all were enormously distant, Michel thought he could at least begin to distinguish types. Those of the military somehow moved a little differently, radiating a different blend of energies, even here in the gravitational deeps of the solar system where nothing like full interstellar speed could safely be attained.

A few meters from where Michel drifted amid his small bodyguard of technicians, suited, watchful and mostly silent, the scoutship that was to pace him on his first circuit of Miranda rested, still docked against the hemispherical bulk of the operations building. Between observations of ships and moons, Michel could switch his attention to what some of the people in the building and the nearby ship were saying. There were a good many words he could not catch, but with every minute of practice there were a few more that he could.

At the moment the most easily recognizable voices were those of Mr. Tupelov and Dr. Iyenari. Relatively near, the two men were supposed to ride the scout during the test but were at the moment exercising what Michel had come to understand was one of the most noticeable privileges of rank, that of keeping other people waiting.

Tupelov's voice said, ". . . still no other successful wearers in the . . . or so . . . possibility of trying to clone him."

Moons and ships dropped out of Michel's thoughts for the moment. He stared at the building's side as if Lancelot might be able to see through that.

Iyenari: ". . . never worked too well, historically . . . Marcus is an example . . ."

Tupelov: ". . . the good colonel out to stud, perhaps . . . follow one order at least without any argument. Then the . . . Michel when he's a little older. Do me a little report . . . speed up his maturation."

Iyenari (with some feeling, only surprise perhaps): ". . . you had started that . . . risky to mess around with . . . hormonal . . . only one we've got. But I'll check it out."

Tupelov: "Do that."

The two men were easier to hear, now, walking toward the scoutship and about to enter it. Michel shifted his gaze back to the sky. Another moon in view now, this one also being overtaken. Would this be Umbriel? Two sets of clumsy feet were entering the scoutship from the building now, men's voices innocently greeting his mother, who had got on ahead of them.

Umbriel, if that was truly its name, occulted a bright nameless star. What would it be like to live on Umbriel? Alone, of course. Except for Lancelot.

Hormonal treatments. He was a little vague about that, but in general he thought he understood.

Presently his mother's face appeared at a cleared port on one side of the scout, and she exchanged waves with her spacedrifting son.

Tupelov, appearing just beside her, now began to speak on radio, using his public voice. "Michel? Today we're going to let you set the pace. Choose your own altitude and direction, but we'd like you to fly completely around Miranda on as direct a route as you can manage. Then if you can, return to this starting point from a direction exactly opposite from that of your departure. We'll just follow and observe. Got that?"

"I understand." Michel had never got into the habit of calling Tupelov "sir," as almost everyone else did. At one time it might have been easy to catch the habit; now it seemed that he never would.

The Secretary had turned away from the port, and was speaking to someone else, in what he must suppose was off-mike privacy: ". . . order of a thousand kilometers, and I'd guess it might take him an hour, based on the kind of velocity he's achieved so far. We'll just have to see. If he gets lost we'll continue observing for a time before we offer help, see how he copes." Back on radio again, Tupelov resumed: "Michel? Any time you're ready."

Michel let his purpose of movement flow into Lancelot. By now this was for him no trickier a process than sending a will to walk into his own legs. His feet brushed the ground, then left it as his body tilted forward, a slow toppling dive that turned into a head-first horizontal acceleration. His arms and legs trailing, his chin slightly raised so that his/Lancelot's eyes could better see what lay ahead, Michel made a silent, fast departure from his starting mark.

He set his flight at an altitude where all but the tallest fingers of the scarred-glass Mirandan landscape were beneath him. Now he could see that the surface skimming by below him was pocked with geometric drifts of some whitish frozen gas. Vaguely impatient, he willed an effortless speed increase. A thousand kilometers, approximately, to go. Should he try to finish the flight in one hour exactly, to the second, just to see what Tupelov's reaction would be? Or maybe in exactly half that time?

The scoutship, in flight as dark and silent as Michel's own, came ghosting after him. Michel let an invisible tendril of Lancelot's being trail where the ship would run into it, an extension of something less than matter and more than thought. It formed a tenuous connection through which Michel could hear another unintended transmission of Dr. Iyenari's voice:

". . . other reason for coming way out to Uranus is of course the isolation."

"Security." That was Michel's mother's voice.

"Yes."

Tupelov's voice put in: "Security's not what I'd like it to be, frankly. Most people even in the government sort of pooh-pooh the goodlife threat in Sol System. But now there are eight billion people living on Earth, and a couple of billion more on Mars and Venus and in the Belts. If only one out of ten thousand had any goodlife tendencies . . . and there are thousands of ships passing in and out of the system daily, and no one really keeps track of all of them . . . "

Michel withdrew his contact from the ship and retreated into his own thoughts. To stay on course needed only a glance ahead from time to time. No one else yet understood how well he had already learned to live with Lancelot.

Concentrating his attention mainly on the ships that he could pick out in interplanetary space, he soon discovered how to make his perception of their drive energies a little plainer than before. Presently he decided that four of them, fairly near and moving very little relative to Uranus, were patrol craft keeping watch on the proving grounds' invisible boundaries. One other ship, smaller, was a little more distant but definitely headed into the Uranian system.

What if he were to abandon the test, and instead

fly out a million kilometers or so to meet one of those ships? The people aboard would goggle at him through their screens and ports, and wonder also at the scoutship full of angry radio voices on his tail. His mother would, of course, be horrendously upset. But there would be nothing much that Tupelov could do. . . .

One of the patrol craft was now moving toward the small visitor, which perhaps was bringing more important people up from Earth. The two ships seemed to be directly approaching Miranda, though they were not going to get much closer before Michel's own rock-hopping flight dropped them below his small horizon.

Gliding through space, an easy swimmer, he looked back and down at his body in its orange gym suit and vague gauze that fluttered as if with wind. Hormone treatments would mean some kind of chemicals to make him grow and develop faster. Maybe, after all, that wouldn't be a bad idea. The faster he grew, the sooner he would be able to protect himself.

Ahead of him now loomed a cone of rock ten meters high, a real Mirandan mountain. Lancelot felt the obstacle coming in plenty of time for Michel to glance ahead and alter course. Like a darting fish he flashed around the rock, and on an impulse he picked up speed in the same instant. He wondered if he could, today, outmaneuver Frank's scoutship in a game of hide and seek.

But he didn't really want to contend against Frank any more, or make Frank mad at him. Here came Oberon, right overhead, the intricate orbital dance of Uranus' attendants turning the satellite momentarily retrograde against the stars.

Six flashes of light, intense bright pinpoints, appeared on Oberon's dark flank.

Six flashes that were answered by five streaks,

five dingy-looking tracer bullets fired along five clustered paths. The streaks began in space somewhere above Miranda, between the two satellites, and headed unerringly back to the original flashpoints on black Oberon. Halfway there, the five were joined and completed by the sixth.

It took only a moment for Michel's memory to find and extract the understanding that he needed, from descriptions in the space-war stories of his childhood. He had just seen six ships or missiles fired from supposedly deserted Oberon. Six *things*, that, as soon as they had effectively cleared the Oberonian surface, started toward Miranda at a speed effectively faster than light. They must have moved in a series of c-plus microjumps, so that the light emitted by them at mid-course reached Michel's eyes before that radiated earlier, causing the appearance of backward movement. Six things had been launched toward Miranda at a speed almost suicidal this deep inside a gravitational system, one of them indeed destroyed by its own reckless speed midway, five of them obviously slowing to some extent, or they would be here now. . . .

Michel had not yet altered his own flight. But the scoutship that had been following him was now suddenly bulking almost against him, forcing him with delicate precision to change his flight path, urging him almost against the jagged rock that sped below. From inside the scout he could hear the fright in his mother's voice, the anger in Tupelov's, both raised in unbelieving protest against their newly clumsy pilot.

Frank, his volume turned up, easily overrode them both. "Michel, get in." The order was bellowed, but still delivered with serenity, with happiness.

Simultaneously the scoutship's entry hatch,

already positioned almost exactly before Michel, snapped open like a fish's jaw. Obediently he slid inside, and the hatch had closed on him again before it occurred to him to wonder whether Frank might possibly, for once, be wrong. Frank of course knew a lot, but where Lancelot was concerned only Michel himself really knew. . . . The scout was accelerating, smooth but ferocious power piling up gravities that Michel could sense despite his cushioning against them. The sealing outer hatch had actually closed on a portion of Lancelot's robe train, which now slid in anyway without a tug. He was going to have to get inside where the others were right away and talk to Frank—

Horrendous shock came, slamming the scoutship in a direction that had to be down, because initial shock was followed a millisecond later by a crumpling impact of the hull against Mirandan rock. Somewhere inside the inner airlock door, Michel's mother was screaming, and he knew that her arms were reaching out with an instinct to protect her baby. But there was no protection there inside the ship for him, and none for her while he was near. Michel had to draw away from her the forces that were coming to kill him, and he saw now that he dared trust his own survival to nothing and no one save Lancelot.

He touched the switch to open the outer airlock door, and despite the jolting it had received a moment ago the mechanism responded promptly. In an instant Michel was out, and even as his buffered feet touched rock, the door was slammed shut again behind him. Frank was wrenching the scoutship back up into space, where it vanished at once from Michel's perception in a sky gone white with an artificial storm of weapons radiation. Miranda's automated defenses, whatever they might be, had opened up. The enemy was here in force; a fight was on.

The shockwave of some explosion, no more than a thin wall of expanding gas, caught Michel up like a butterfly and hurled him across the jagged glass of a landscape that he could not feel with Lancelot insulating him from injury. He floated for long moments in a blind, deaf void. Intermittent flashes of the Mirandan surface came to him, as if by lightning's illumination, and were immediately wiped away to nothingness again. He understood that all-too-efficient protection was guarding his senses against annihilation; somehow there ought to be a way to make Lancelot let in just enough sensory input to carry information. . . .

Groping for controls that were, as usual, within himself, Michel managed an adjustment. When the world came back, he found himself crouching on all fours, surrounded by boiling rock in molten puddles. Around him in the poor gravity gobs of lava drifted, like one-celled organisms. Under a bridge made by his gloveless fingers, a red-hot crevice in some solider material jetted smoke and flames at gunshot velocity.

Above his head the thunderstorms of weaponry still raged. He ought to fly for shelter, find help, try to attack the enemy, do something, but he had no idea of which way to turn for any of these purposes. Simply flying up into the melee above would be as pointless and perhaps as dangerous as jumping into the teeth of a ripsaw. He crouched motionless, listening in desperation. At last he could make out, under the continued battle noise, that a new network of intense radio communication had been established, among many stations unfamiliar to him. Messages were being sent and answered at superhuman speed, in what sounded like no human code that he had ever heard.

What must be a detector beam of some kind came fingering at him. It went away, then came back to lock on.

Michel sprang to his feet. As in a nightmare, from a childhood that now could be no more, he ran. He sprinted in blind panic, his tentative plans and even the powers of Lancelot forgotten for the moment. A drifting cloud of boulders loomed ahead, jarred up in the fighting and weightless as bubbles in feeble Miranda's grip. Panic drove Michel right in among the great rock masses, trying to lose himself. As he ran directly beneath a house-sized chunk of glowing slag, Michel suddenly found himself with no surface at all beneath his feet. In desperate fear he reached at last for active aid from Lancelot. Arms thrust forward like a diver's, he flew among stone masses that closed him between them into darkness, momentary peace. He slid between a thousand tons on either side, feeling no more than a brushing, as by enormous pillows, as Lancelot's delicate fringes ground away the rock.

He was out in free space again. Ahead, a cloud of smaller fragments beckoned, and he flew into it as quickly as he could. Now he/Lancelot was at last alone, the enemy's radio gabble for the moment left behind. On other wavelengths he could now distinguish chattering human voices. Help was going to come for him, eventually . . . if he could survive until it did.

The respite allowed his mind to surface from its panic, for a gasp of sanity and an attempt at planning. Should he stay where he was, or keep moving? He was disoriented; he no longer knew in which direction the operations building lay. Nor was he certain that he ought to try to reach it.

There came a great blast in the middle distance, and the wave of gases from it started a quick dispersal of Michel's protective cloud of debris. The human radio talk was blown away as well, to be replaced by a fresh flow of enemy code.

A locator beam flicked at him again. This time he could pinpoint its source, less than a hundred meters off. Something not human was moving there, picking its deliberate way toward him.

He launched himself at once, at top speed, in the opposite direction. Behind him a throng of pursuers came on at the speed of racing aircraft, things human-sized but of the wrong shape to be human, jetting and bounding over the black and broken surface. Michel managed an acceleration, and the enemy momentarily fell behind. But their signals beaming past him now were answered, from above him and from in front.

He halted his flight, braced Lancelot's feet as well as he could upon the surface. Hard-edged shapes were closing in upon him from all sides. Blind panic clutched at Michel again, but with a great effort he eluded it, escaping through an inward door. Lancelot bore him into the domain whose borders Michel had only glimpsed before, during the last fractal second of his sparring match with Frank. Time hardened into an almost motionless sea carved out of congealed energy.

With this altered perception he saw a hard inhuman arm come reaching for him. Then they were not out to kill him, after all . . . they wanted something else. Through Lancelot's fields the contact of the arm felt infinitely less human than the touch of the steel that Frank had sometimes brushed him with. Michel poured toughness into his own right arm's extension, and with a motion enormously pure and swift he knocked the approaching limb away. He could see the details of the metal gripper that formed the berserker android's hand, watch it recede with what appeared to be infinite slowness, then as slowly start to swing back again.

Meanwhile another faceless machine-shape had jumped almost within reach. Michel, with no sense that he was hurrying, turned to face it. His forefingers were raised and pointing, in a gesture that his conscious mind had never planned. A fierce flow from his fingertips exploded blindingly and a metal form vanished in radii of molten ceramics and burned metal. But already another berserker stood at his other side, arms reaching for him. They could move as quickly as he could, and they were going to win.

Not yet. Again a pointing finger bore his will. Along the interface between Michel's own mind and the entity called Lancelot, his terror and rage and hate were melded with the power of fusing hydrogen nuclei. Again a blast came, shattering machines and armor.

But always more grippers, and still more, came reaching for him. The whole horde was close upon him now. With carefulness as great and inhuman as their strength and speed they closed their hands upon his neck, his legs, one arm. Yet somehow (Michel himself could not perceive it happening) Lancelot once more fought him free, and bore him away into a close orbit of Miranda, at speeds Michel had never before attempted. Space was barred to him, the sky in all directions dominated by the great machines of the enemy, victorious for the moment. But this was the proving grounds, Sol System, and massive help had to be on the way. . . .

Unexcited and unworried, the hornets' droning of the berserker androids' radio voices followed in his flight. The operations building loomed up suddenly before Michel and he braked to a stop. All of the structure's defensive shields, mirror-shiny and insubstantial in appearance, had been erected. Atop the shields, fifteen meters above Miranda's crack-ruined rock, a metal giant squatted, dull monster on a silver toadstool. It was hunched in a position that meant that all its might was bent on forcing a way down into its perch.

Will you fight against berserkers, little one?

Yelling to one another in their clipped radio bursts, shifting formation in perfect teamwork, the pack of Michel's surviving pursuers caught up with him again.

Again Lancelot guided him into the realm that seemed to lie beyond time. And now Michel began for the first time to feel dully the stresses that Lancelot could impose upon a connected human mind. A feeling of unreality sapped his will, even as exhaustion dragged at his muscles. He grappled with a steel berserker arm, and saw and felt it bending in his grip, metal rupturing in the grip of Lancelot. Then something heavier tangled his own arms, his neck—a net of some kind, its strands burning with fierce energies that he was not going to be allowed the time to solve.

Still, somehow, Lancelot had him halfway through the net before the machines surrounding him could manage to bring the escaping motion to a halt. Too many active weights were on him now, too many devices gripping; he could not bend or break or blast them all.

He heard a shrill and childish voice, his own, go screaming out across the void. Then a thing with the strength of a log-hauler pulled Lancelot's legs out from under him, and under all the weights his shielded face was slammed against Mirandan rock.

With all the powers that he knew how to draw

from Lancelot, Michel strained in a last effort to get free. A meter before his eyes, a berserker's legs had been somehow drilled into rock for greater purchase. The legs pulled out now, rock shattering as Lancelot tore them free. But still, with its cohort's help, the pinning berserker held.

Michel's awareness, now somewhere on the far side of panic, remained clear through it all. They had him pinned at last, and now they were inflating over him something that proved to be a plastic bubble holding air.

In the distance there were still flashes of radiation, rock-shuddering jolts that told of an ongoing fight. But there was no signal of approaching help as yet, and now help was going to come too late. With great deftness his captors' metal fingers were searching out the fastenings of Lancelot. They found them, one by one, and with a motherlike gentleness they severed Michel/Lancelot in half.

NINE

EVEN WHILE ITS OWN INTERNAL ANALYTICAL SYSTEMS were still working with the sample of blood from the femal life-unit, the Co-ordinator ordered itself moved to the control room of the goodlife ship. There it established itself in direction control of all important ship's systems. A few nanoseconds' difference in reaction time could be crucial in space combat, and the odds were overwhelming that intense space combat was imminent. The badlife proving grounds could not be so nearly defenseless as they seemed. But the Co-ordinator was going to have powerful help. Its programming informed it that the time was at hand when all available reserves must be risked in an attempt to take control of or destroy the life-unit designated Michel Geulincx.

From the start of its long, clandestine journey to Sol System, the Co-ordinator had carried in its unliving memory detailed information on every known local resource that it might be able to call upon for help when it arrived. The resources that made the present plan look feasible were the combat units that had long ago been hidden on Oberon, in anticipation of the day when Sol System itself could be successfully attacked. Six berserker fighting ships of intermediate class, with their auxiliary robots and machines, had been secretly cached there decades before the badlife had established their proving grounds in the same region. The six ships had originally been intended, by the master berserker computers sometimes known to humanity as the Directors, to form one small squadron of the armada required for a successful assault on Earth itself. But now the Directors' agent had been instructed that seizure of Michel Geulincx had as high a priority as destruction of the badlife homeworld itself.

Correct timing was, as usual, essential. The possibly valuable female captive was secured in a cabin—all records of human behavior indicated that immature life-units such as Michel Geulincx were often greatly dependent upon parental units. The possibly-still-valuable goodlife units were assigned chairs, protected by emergency webbings, in the control room. The berserker, now in complete control of the ship, ignored the signals of the human guard-ship that had now begun a moderately fast course of interception. In a range of frequencies that ranged from light to radio waves the Co-ordinator fired toward Oberon a quick burst of code, information enormously condensed. This message roused the sleeping fighters hidden there and at the same time programmed them with the tactical necessities of the new situation.

The battle following, most of it fought on and around the Mirandan surface, was sharp but short. With an electronic analog of satisfaction, the Co-ordinator observed the rapid disabling of local resistance. The patrol craft were beaten off, the one spaceborne scoutship knocked down and crippled, the operations building effectively isolated inside the stubborn knot of its automated defenses. It would be hours before the very large human forces routinely posted elsewhere in Sol System could reach the scene. Indeed, it would be hours before they knew that anything was amiss.

With the Michel Geulincx unit captured, as well as the weapons system it had been using, both life-unit and weapon appearing essentially undamaged, the Co-ordinator had achieved the highest-priority goals for which it had been programmed. To remain near Miranda for even the short time necessary to expunge all remaining life from the satellite would have meant risking this great success, as very strong and persistent pursuit had to be expected. Therefore the Co-ordinator ordered immediate departure. In the center of a protective formation made up of the three surviving berserker warcraft, the goodlife ship under the Co-ordinator's direct control departed the Uranian system at maximum practical acceleration and roughly in the direction of solar north, along a line where it could be computed that interception would be least probable.

As the goodlife aboard were instructed to divest themselves of acceleration harness, a premature celebration broke out among them, which the Co-ordinator at once quelled with a few spoken words. There was no time; there was business that needed urgently to be conducted and in which their help would be used. It was possible that the weapons system code-named Lancelot had been designated to self-destruct somehow when captured. Or it might rapidly deteriorate from some other cause. Therefore an immediate examination of the system, and some preliminary testing of it, was essential.

Even cushioned in a berth and isolated in a cabin, Elly Temesvar had no difficulty in recognizing a space battle when the ship in which she rode was thrust into the middle of one. The timing and the roughness of the c-plus jumps were unmistakable, as were the sounds with which the hull around her rang. They were certainly not the sounds of a routine boarding from an armed patrol craft, which was what she had been expecting.

Before being introduced to the Co-ordinator, she had thought herself to be in the hands of a small group of people of psychotic audacity but quite limited intelligence. The presence of an authentic berserker as their leader changed these estimates completely. Still, it had seemed almost incredible that her captors should have on call enough armed force to mount a successful raid against the Uranian proving grounds—this was Sol System, after all!

But there was no denying what she heard and felt. While the hull still rang with nearby shooting, there came an additional grating vibration that told Elly the ship was down on the rocky surface of some Uranian satellite. Airlocks were cycled and recycled several times. Minutes later, the fighting died away, and with a last scraping of her hull the goodlife vessel was off into space again, on what course Elly had no way of guessing. Then her heart sank as human voices, the goodlife voices on the ship, were raised in a brief burst of jubilation.

After a timeless interval of apparently peaceful flight, the door to Elly's prison-cabin was opened once again. Without surprise, but still with a shock that seemed almost to stop her heart, she saw a man-sized robot enter. Through her mind passed images, not entirely repellent, of quick death. Her pale body thrown out from an airlock . . .

But the machine was not killing her. After undoing the ties that held her to the bunk, it simply stood back, gesturing with one human-shaped hand toward the open door. She got to her feet and on uncertain legs moved the other way instead, toward the cabin's small sanitary alcove. It did not stop her, but it followed closely, staying within reach of her and watching her every movement closely.

Having her privacy violated by a machine was not at all the same as suffering the same offense from a human being, though in some obscure way she felt it ought to be. The discovery that her fate was not, after all, to be instant death was enough to make her a little giddy with relief. She kept the thing waiting a moment longer while she rinsed her hands and got a drink of water. Then she offered no argument or resistance when it took her by the wrist and tugged her out into the narrow corridor. Their flight was still steady and smooth, the artificial gravity constant. For most of the short walk to the control room the machine that led Elly followed another, similar robot. This one was carrying a small human form, fair-haired, in an orange costume of some kind. At her first glimpse of the face, Elly thought: The boy from the picture. At least there was a considerable resemblance.

Her own biological son? Michel? It must be, if any of this was going to make sense. But the idea aroused no feeling at all within her.

The small ship's control room was somewhat larger than Elly had expected. It had room for six

humans, two goodlife women and two men standing crowded together. The second woman was
dark, with an Oriental face, much thinner than she
who had visited Elly in the cabin. Seeing the goodlife together, Elly was struck by the idea that they
all looked somehow sexless; more than that, inhuman, though exactly what gave her this impression in each case was more than she could think
out now.

Michel was in the room also, still in the grip of
the machine that had been carrying him, though
the boy's feet were on the deck now and he appeared to be able to stand unaided. His dazed
child's eyes brushed Elly's, but she could see no
reaction in them.

In the center of the chamber, the Co-ordinator
now rode on top of the ship captain's control console, presenting an image, no doubt unintentional,
of a huge spider on a stump, bound in place by a
connective complex of wires and cabling. Directly
before it, draped as though carelessly across the
otherwise empty captain's chair, lay folds of
something that looked at first glance like large
sheets of loosely crumpled, almost transparent
gauze.

For a few moments after Elly's arrival, the tab-
leau held in silence. The goodlife, unrestrained by
machines, seemed to be waiting humbly, perhaps
with just a trace of boredom, and Elly was reminded momentarily of some of the gatherings for
services in the Temple. Then a wordless order
must have been given by the Co-ordinator. The robot holding Elly dropped her wrist and moved to
the chair before the console. There it deliberately
picked up the gauze in one of its almost human
hands. Only now did Elly notice that its other hand
depended from a badly damaged arm. The bone-
shaped upper arm had been crippled and bent

somehow, the metal surface ruptured. In the recent fighting, no doubt. What kind of weapon,
though, would have produced . . . ?

The Co-ordinator's squeaky voice was speaking,
and to her: "Life-unit Temesvar, you will identify
this weapons system."

Taken unawares, Elly looked around the cabin
desperately, thinking that she must have missed
something somehow. Then she saw that the eyes
of the goodlife were all focused on the gauze.
"That—stuff, on the chair? Is it some kind of body
shield, then? I know nothing about it. It's been
many years since I've dealt with weapons." She
felt surprise and a touch of shame at her own eagerness for survival, her willingness to answer the
Co-ordinator as fully as possible.

The Co-ordinator said: "Life-unit Michel Geulincx. Answer."

The boy's eyes had begun to study Elly's face,
and they continued to do so even as he replied to
the berserker. He did not seem terribly afraid;
perhaps he was still too dazed by what must have
been the awesome shock of capture. He said, "It's
what we call Lancelot . . . you must already know
that."

There was a silent pause. The goodlife, just a
little restless, continued waiting. Michel turned
his gaze from Elly toward the machine that was
eventually going to order them all killed.

Then a new order was evidently given, at some
non-human level. The man-sized robot with the
crippled arm, moving slowly but with great deftness despite its disability, began putting on the
gauze sheets. It dressed itself like an actor with
an unfamiliar cloak, or perhaps a skeleton trying
on an unfamiliar wedding dress. The folds of what
it put on went swirling slowly, fading with distance from the wearer. From solid reality where

they embraced the robot's body, they passed into invisibility at a couple of meters' distance. They were complex forcefields, obviously, though of exactly what kind, Elly could not begin to guess.

. . . the badlife have grasped at least the fact that he is unusual, and they mean to use him as part of a weapons system. Have you ever heard the code name Lancelot?

With the strange gauze now fastened more or less firmly to its torso and its head, the robot began to move about a little. Gently, with a certain skeletal engineering grace, it stepped and postured. To Elly's mind there came the image of a Dance of Death that she had seen somewhere.

Michel's small gasp, a couple of meters to her left, broke in upon her fascinated concentration. The boy was staring at the robot with an expression Elly could not read. She looked back at the grotesquely draped machine herself, and watched it several seconds longer before it was borne in upon her that something about the test was going badly.

The robot's good hand had moved to one of the fasteners on its chest, as if it might be going to tear itself free of what it had put on, but could not quite make up its electronic mind to do so. The damaged arm meanwhile rose in an astonishingly human gesture, flapping a useless hand and forearm across its own head as if in madness or dismay. Then, stiffly as a toppled statue, the machine fell to the deck in an abrupt swirl of gauze.

Two others of its kind were at its side at once. With hands moving faster than human eyes could follow, they manipulated fastenings, stripping away the slow-billowing robes from the inert body, which remained inert even when they were done.

The Co-ordinator itself gave no evidence of having been affected in the least. "On human volunteer," it presently called out.

Four human hands were raised. Stal's hand, Elly noticed, came up just a little less promptly than the others.

"Life-unit Mabuchi," uttered the machine. The stocky deacon stepped forward, and reached to take up the strange garment from where it had been replaced upon the chair. His eyes were rounded with an emotion that Elly read as a blend of ecstasy and fear.

Then he snatched his hand back as if it had been burned, when the berserker startled him by speaking again: "You will put on Lancelot. Having done so, you will then not move or act in any way except at my direct command."

"Yes, lord and master." The deacon's answer was so low that Elly lip-read rather than heard it. Quite psychotic, she thought, looking at the man's rapt face. Why didn't I ever see that in him in the Temple?

Mabuchi hesitated about his gray smock, then eventually decided to leave the garment on as the robots began to help him fit the shimmering stage-wrappings over it. At first Elly thought that his head remained uncovered, but then she caught a glimpse of haze that clung round his dark-haired cranium like a ghostly helmet.

The machines, finished with their task, stepped back, but no more than one small step each. Mabuchi's eyes were closed now, and like a newly blind man he put out his hands with fingers groping. He seemed to be listening intently to something that Elly could not hear.

Then his eyes opened, his lips moved. "Am I dying?" he asked of the company in general, in a voice that now sounded like that of a man trying to be cunning rather than submissive.

"I detect no evidence of—"

The rest of the Co-ordinator's reply was lost, as Mabuchi suddenly lunged toward the central console where it perched. The machines on his right and left immediately seized both his arms, and behind him another robot materialized from somewhere, holding in both hands a glowing net. But—Elly could not see how—the deacon's right arm was suddenly free again. Growling strange noises, he struck with it at the robot on his left. His fingers, like the paw of a clawing animal draped in suddenly glowing gauze, struck the machine across the front of its head. The area that in a human would have been the face was wiped away, turned into a molten smear as if it had been soft putty.

The glowing net had enveloped Mabuchi now, and the two robots still standing fought him to a standstill while he screamed. One of the last undid the fastening of Lancelot at the deacon's throat, and the gauze helm was peeled back from his head. A crackling echo filled the small room, marking the passage of something moving at shockwave speeds; Elly saw a black hole the diameter of a pencil leap into existence in the center of the deacon's forehead. His fleshy body sagged in the metal arms of the machines he fought. He twitched a few times and was still.

A small hatch closed softly in the middle of the Co-ordinator's casing. Elly turned her eyes toward the boy who was supposed to be her son. Michel was watching her again; there was fright in his face now, but a busy intelligence was there also. Did he have any idea of who she was?

Before she could decide whether or not to try to speak to him, a machine had come and was pulling her away. As she was tugged out of the control room into the passage again, she turned her head for a last look at her son.

Augmentation gravity in the operations building was almost gone, along with a lot of other things. But the life support systems were still functioning in an emergency mode. And a number of people were still around to breathe the air the systems fed them.

Tupelov was talking, to the surviving human operator at the surviving Moonbase ticker: "Tell the admiral to bypass us completely here for now. The attack here is definitely over. We have functioning life-systems and some functioning ships. Tell him get everything into pursuit and interception."

"Sir, if you would—"

"I'm busy. I've told them once. You tell them." He didn't want to get into planning discussions now; he didn't want to get into lengthy conversation with the President; once that happened he would be given orders and he would be stuck. What Tupelov had to decide first concerned an option that he hadn't mentioned to anyone else as yet—whether it might be best to gather what ships he had at the proving grounds and join in the pursuit personally.

He walked across the great room, an odd-looking place in the emergency lighting mode, swaying up high on his toes in the low g. As always when he found himself in a prolonged low-g situation, he was going to have to struggle against spacesickness. Coming to his present goal, another emergency communications station, Tupelov gripped a railing in search of visceral support.

"Is Colonel Marcus back yet? What'd he get?" Marcus, you had to give him that, was really very good at most of the parts of his job that really mattered. After getting the crippled scout and the people in it back to base somehow, the Colonel had rolled his boxes right into another craft and had immediately headed out from Miranda in a dangerous series of c-plus microjumps, planning to reach a distance from which the raid of two hours earlier could be photographed as it took place.

"He's back, sir. Want to talk to him?"

"No. Just run me whatever he got." And Tupelov gratefully threw himself into a chair, which helped the low-g queasies somewhat. On a small stage before him, three-dimensional pictures almost immediately began to run.

"They came from Oberon. God damn." Tupelov watched as, in jumpy, computer-enhanced magnification, the six berserker craft came hurtling in, one of them destroyed en route by a backlash from tortured space itself. They had known exactly where they were going, all right, and had risked all to get there before they could be stopped.

Someone was standing beside his chair, and he knew without looking back that it was Carmen. Neither of them said anything as they watched the recorded light flare out and back across the Mirandan surface.

Now came the part where the robotic photointerpreters had to strain their limits, trying to show what had happened to one small figure in an orange suit. A dot, surrounded in the small pictures by pursuing machines. The machines closed in, and then the dot was out from among them somehow. *What a weapon.*

"Is my boy still alive? Can you tell me that much at least?"

It took a few seconds for her words to seep through his intense concentration upon the ongoing struggle. No sooner had the finally-captured dot been hauled aboard the goodlife ship than it and its friends had blasted off. "No, I can't," said Tupelov, brutally.

Carmen surprised him then, moving around in front of him so that her body cut off his line of sight to the stage. "Are you hurt?" Tupelov demanded abruptly; she was dragging around in the low-g like some semighostly victim of internal bleeding.

"I want to know," she demanded, "what you're going to do to find my son. They took him, didn't they? Took him alive."

"Get out of my way."

"You tell me."

"Get her out of here!" Tupelov ordered loudly. But then, before the people who came to pull at Carmen had hauled her more than a few meters, he turned his head and called, "Carmen, I'm betting he's still alive. I'm going to do everything I can to get him back. Everything. I mean it."

Carmen must have heard him, but did not answer. More collapsed than not, she let herself be taken off.

Before Tupelov could start to rerun the pictures, a young woman aide came up to his side in a bounding ballet run. "Sir? The President is on the ticker. Insists on a personal report from you. And Mr. Lombok has finally been located. Drugged. He's in a hospital on Earth."

Tupelov said out loud what ought to be done to and with the President. On his way back across the big room, bouncing helplessly on his toes, as if in some kind of insane elation, the Secretary passed an improvised alcove where Colonel Marcus had his space suit boxes drawn up, and was talking to debriefers: ". . . he was calling *me* right there at the end, before they took him off. You know, that gets me somehow."

TEN

Even deprived of Lancelot, Michel could feel that the speed of the small goodlife ship was very high as it fled from Miranda. And as soon as the flight was fairly under way he noticed that, as on *Johann Karlsen*, the artificial gravity of this ship had been set at precisely surface normal for Alpine.

When the robot put on Lancelot in the control room, Michel felt certain ahead of time that the machine was not going to be able to survive, and he nursed hopes that the destruction would prove contagious, wiping out the Co-ordinator also. But that device had disconnected itself from its slave before the trial, and Michel's hopes were dashed.

He had not expected the goodlife man to succeed either, of course, and the violent death came as no great surprise to Michel. Though he had in a sense felt death before, he had never seen it, but at the moment it meant almost nothing to him.

Only that one more enemy had been removed, and that the Co-ordinator had sustained a small defeat.

Since he himself was not yet dead, the berserkers obviously hoped for something more than death from him, and he was waiting to discover what. After the stocky goodlife man was shot down, the blond woman the machines did not trust was led out of the control room. She reminded Michel somewhat of his mother, and the thought of his mother dead back on Miranda kept him for a little while from thinking about anything else.

Shortly a few words from the Co-ordinator sent the three surviving goodlife on their way, apparently unguarded. The dead man was stripped carefully out of Lancelot by the surviving machines, and was then dumped like so much garbage into a disposal unit. There was not room for his legs until his upper body had been silently digested, somewhere down inside.

Now Lancelot lay draped across the captain's chair again. The three robots still in the room, their tasks completed for the moment, ceased to move, becoming almost inert machinery. Now Michel was alone at last with the Co-ordinator.

He had been standing through it all, and now he moved to a chair—not the captain's, of course—and sat down, facing the thing that squatted like a great spider on the console.

Having sat down, he waited. The other waited, too. In the great new quiet that seemed to be thickening in the control room, Michel listened for any sound that might be coming from his chief enemy, but could hear nothing. It was so quiet that he thought that with some effort he might now manage to hear his own heart beat, even without the help of Lancelot.

How long he waited thus he did not know. Fear

came back at him in waves, and he fought it back, trying to defend his sanity. Eventually he felt that he was going to succeed in this at least.

No sooner was he sure of this than the berserker spoke. Had it been monitoring his heartbeat also?

It said: "I offer you an end of fear."

"You mean kill me."

"No. I compute that you already know that I mean something else." After allowing him time for an answer he did not make, it went on: "The badlife who have been using you would kill you at this moment if they could. Is it not true?"

"Probably." The thought hadn't struck him till this moment, but it struck hard now.

"But they cannot reach you. I will protect you from them."

"What'll you do with me?"

"I will take you to a place of safety, where you will have a long and happy life."

He doubted that. "Why?"

"You are to be studied because of your unique qualities. But the study will be non-destructive. Kind and gentle and considerate. Your uniqueness must not be damaged and it may be fragile."

"What happened to the other people?" Michel burst out suddenly. "I mean those back on Miranda."

"It is probable that many still survive. To kill them was not my prime objective."

"What about those in the scoutship? The one that was flying near me when I ... I ..."

"It was damaged but not destroyed. Why does that concern you? Those life-units are all your enemies now."

"My—my mother was on that ship." And as Michel spoke he could feel a small though abrupt change in the inertial space his body occupied;

c-plus flight had now begun in earnest. Pursuit by human forces would be a much more difficult problem now, though not yet impossible. Not if the adventure books were right.

The berserker had paused, as if it needed time to compute its next choice of words. "Your mother," it told him now, "is the female life-unit inside whose body your body was formed. That life-unit is aboard this ship. You have seen her in this room."

Michel could feel no impact from mere words just now, whatever they might say. Turning the berserker's last statement over in his mind, he could find no proof that it was untrue. He had long known that he was adopted, and he had heard somewhere that on Alpine at least an effort was generally made to match adoptive to biological parents, even in physical appearance. And there was no doubt that the woman he had just seen looked like his mother. But, supposing the berserker had told the truth, what did it matter now?

It was not going to try to convince him, at least not now. Instead it asked: "When did you first try on the device called Lancelot?"

Sometime, maybe, after he had had a chance to think things out, he would try to lie to it. Right now he saw no need to do so. "Only a few days ago," he answered.

"Where?"

"At Moonbase."

"What were the effects of that first test on you?"

"On me? Not much of anything." Michel's hands were gripping the chair arms hard, but not as hard as he had gripped them on first sitting down a few minutes ago. He could feel muscles in his back shuddering, trying to start to relax.

"And what were the effects upon you of the astragalus and the ring?"

"The what?" Yet in his memory the faintest trace lay, almost buried. Something overhead: *The astragalus is* . . .

The berserker was not going to insist on anything just now. It asked: "And where were you before you went to Moonbase?"

"On Alpine. That's a planet way in near the—"

"Why were you chosen to wear Lancelot?"

"I guess because other people tended to go crazy. You saw. They tried a lot of people." Now Michel could feel microjumps, and multiplying in length as well as frequency. If only he had a cleared port or a screen . . . but what good would that do him?

"Explain the meaning of the designation Lancelot."

He tried to recall just what he had been told on that subject, by some people at Moonbase. "It's the name of a man in some old stories, a famous fighter. Back in the days when men fought with big knives and rode around on animals. Only one other man could ever beat him. His son."

"Do you wish to see your mother now?"

For just an instant Michel's nerves gave a great leap. Then he remembered who the machine meant. "You mean the woman . . . who was here."

"I have told you she is your mother."

"I—yes, I'd like to talk to her."

The robots went into smooth motion once again. A door opened, and again Michel's heart leaped, though only momentarily, at the sight of the tall blonde woman standing in the corridor beyond.

Aboard a larger ship, also thrumming subliminally with its increasing speed of flight, Tupelov occupied a combat chair in a prominent position on the bridge. Carmen sat in a chair beside his. With the seats' protective devices at the moment folded away, she could almost but not quite lean her head on his shoulder. Her posture was half that of a supplicant, half tired lover.

She said, "I heard you give that order for the fleet not to pursue directly any longer, to try for an interception."

"Well, I did. We should have a better chance that way. Another force is going to take up the pursuit, you see, following what they can pick up of the trail as long as they can. A ship jumping does leave a trail of sorts, you know."

"But how can we intercept them if we don't know where they're taking him?"

Across the center of the bridge, surrounded by officers' chairs, a complex display of the whole known galaxy was etched in light, a model of a volume tens of thousands of light years in diameter. Tupelov had spent most of the time since his task force departed the proving grounds in looking at this display, and he was looking at it now. "I'm making my best guess, that's all." He glanced at her briefly. "You look very tired."

"I am. But grateful that you let me come along."

Looking back at the display, Tupelov muttered, "I think there's a definite chance that you'll be useful." He wasn't saying how large a chance. "Why don't you go see the quartermaster, now while things are slow? You've had those same clothes on for two or three days."

She looked down at herself. Since the day of the attack. Twice she had slept in the same garments, and got up thinking she had to do something about a change, and then had completely forgotten such non-essentials. "All right, I'll get something new," she said now, stirring wearily. "Guessing, is that the best we can do?"

He gave her what she thought was a strange look, and said, "It's something I'm very good at, usually. Just as other people are good at other ways of fighting."

"Guessing is guessing, isn't it?"

Tupelov seemed to come to a decision. Forgetting the great display for the moment, he reached to unlock a small drawer in the console before him. "Have you heard anything about these? Rumors concerning them, maybe? They were brought back by Elly Temesvar and Frank Marcus, from the place we call the Taj. If these two items prove anything at all, and I believe they do, it's that chance and guessing and physical laws are really a lot different from what we currently think they are."

The two items rested innocently enough in Carmen's palm. One of them was a small almost-cube with neatly rounded edges. Its material looked and felt to her like bone. Each of its six practically flat sides bore a pattern of unevenly incised dots, not greatly different from those on any ordinary gaming die. The other artifact was a plain metal ring, a little too big for any but the largest human fingers.

"I don't see what . . ."

Tupelov took the die from her palm. "We call this the astragalus," he said. "After a kind of knuckle-bone used in ancient times for gaming." He rolled the thing out on the flat tabletop of the console before them. It came to rest with the single-dot side uppermost. He rolled once more with the same result. Again. Again.

"A kind of loaded die?" Carmen asked.

"No. At least it's not loaded by anything physical, anything that our instruments are capable of discovering. Its balance is such that it should come down according to the laws of probability, like any other fair die. But it's not fair, either. Every fair trial brings the one-dot side up on top."

"*Every* trial?"

He rolled it again, in demonstration.

"And what about the ring?" Carmen turned the tiny circlet this way and that between her fingers, then let it rest once more in her palm.

"I wouldn't put it on my finger. Though that's been tried, too, without apparent effect. . . . Look carefully at the finish around the outer edge. Anything strike you as remarkable?"

When she moved the ring between her fingers again, Carmen noticed that the surface of the rim sometimes seemed to blur, as if it could be moving at a different speed from the material beneath. This flow or slippage ceased immediately when she once more held the artifact still. She described what she saw as best she could to Tupelov, adding, "But I'm sure that could be produced in a number of ways by our own technology. Is that what you meant?"

"No. But it appears to have some connection with the real oddity, which it took us some time to discover. And which is that the ring you're holding has a circumference which always measures just three times its measured diameter."

It took Carmen a moment to understand; then she remarked that the ring appeared to be perfectly circular.

"Oh, it is, by any other test. But pi, for this ring, equals exactly three. Very simple, and very simply impossible." When Carmen couldn't find a comment, he went on, "Get something to measure it with, later, and you can try for yourself."

He reclaimed the ring from her hand now, and put both artifacts away. Then, looking at the display again, he said, "Michel, in a sense, came from the same place that those things did. He was conceived there, and then sent out into the world. Our world."

A new kind of fear dug into Carmen, somewhere deep inside. "What do you mean?"

"I hardly know myself what I mean. Consider the artifacts. On the surface, they seem normal. Whatever the basis of their peculiarity is, we can't measure it or detect it. All they do is make hash of our picture of the universe as a place defined by the laws of physics and probability we have discovered. Like—like some kind of educational toys that have been given to us. To make us use our intelligence. Or—"

"Or what?"

"To make us use, discover in ourselves perhaps, some other faculty. Or to test us. I don't know—"

"And you're telling me that Michel—came—from this same place? You called it the Taj, just now."

"Yes. He did. Now don't, Carmen, that's not going to help. Therefore my best educated guess is that Michel is now being taken to the Directors; it's a guess, not a logical deduction. Don't, I said. They can't do him any more harm than any other berserker machine can. Anyway I don't think that their intention is to harm him."

Carmen sank back in her chair. Her eyes were closed and her lips had no more color than her skin. "Where are we going, then?"

"We're going to put in at Alpine first, because it's on our way. I want to see what we can pick up there in the way of recent information. Then we're going on, with more ships if I can get the Alpine government to send some with us. To where I believe the Directors are now, and where we can intercept Michel, if anywhere." The Secretary leaned forward, stabbing at the display with a lightpointer. "Right where the Taj was last reported. Right there near the Core."

ELEVEN

AT SOME POINT IN THE JOURNEY, AND IT WAS IN THE very nature of the difficulty that Michel did not know exactly when, he discovered that, at least as far as his conscious mind was concerned, he had lost all track of time. He no longer seemed to have any clear conception of how long ago he had been captured.

He supposed he would be lucky if that was the worst mental damage he suffered from everything that had happened to him so far.

The woman called Elly, with whom Michel was having frequent though still halting conversations, said that yes, she was probably his bio-mother. Somehow they managed not to talk much about that, or indeed much about anything at all. And outside of his meetings with her, his contact with human beings was at a minimum. He was guarded continuously by one or more of the robots, he spent much of his time alone in the small cabin to which he had been assigned. At frequent intervals he was escorted out of his cabin, and allowed to exercise in the ship's tiny gym, where he worked with the springs and weights and the treadmill and the bouncing balls as he was bidden by the machines. Then again he would be taken to the control room, for long periods of gentle questioning by the Co-ordinator. Elly shared the gym with him sometimes, but never the control room sessions, during which one or two of the goodlife people were sometimes present. These usually stood or sat in the background, sometimes looking as if they wished they were somewhere else, never having much to say, ready to let their lord and master do all the talking. Most often it was the metallic-looking man called Stal who sat in on these interviews, and sometimes the stocky young goodlife woman whose name Michel still had not heard. Only on rare occasions did the thinner, more Oriental-looking woman take part. Once, Michel heard Stal call her by the name of Hoshi.

Rare occasions? How many occasions, how many conversations with the Co-ordinator, had there been in all, if a group of more than one of them could be called rare? Michel couldn't remember. Time was getting away from him.

Was it because the berserker was drugging him, or hypnotizing him somehow? After some consideration, Michel didn't think so. He thought that it must want to handle him as delicately as possible, keeping him at Michel-normal if it could, until it got him to where the Directors were waiting to provide him with that long and happy life. He decided, too, that the machine's conversations were intended more as a monitoring of his mental condition than as serious efforts to convert him to willing goodlife status.

"Tell me a story," Michel probed at it once, when there was no one else in the control room.

"What shall the subject of the story be?"

"Goodlife."

After a hesitation lasting only a few seconds, it began. The story it related was a horrible thing, about people who took great risks and underwent great torment at the hands of badlife in order to help some berserker machines slaughter a great number of other people.

"I don't want to hear any more," Michel interrupted firmly. The relation stopped in mid-sentence. Nor was the conversation immediately resumed.

When he was next summoned to the control room, Michel found Stal there with the commanding machine. "Tell Michel of the goodness of being goodlife," the Co-ordinator ordered its living servant.

"Of course." Stal paused briefly, like a man marshaling his thoughts. But Michel got the feeling that the pause, like the speech that came after it, had been rehearsed.

Stal began, "Insofar as life can be good in any sense, it is so only in serving the cause of death."

"Why is death good?" Michel interrupted.

Stal indicated astonishment at the question. His manner seemed to say: If you cannot see that for yourself, nothing that I can say will help. At last he replied, "If you had seen more of life, young sir, you would not ask me that."

"Have you seen much of death?"

"Death is the final goal of us all, the gift of peace. It—"

"But you are still alive, yourself. And the two women."

The gray-white man looked at Michel benignly.

"We are needed, to help in the great cause. For the time being we are denied our rest."

"Co-ordinator?" Michel looked at the machine. "Does this man really want to die?"

Somewhere in the control room, something electronic made the faintest of musical gurgles; otherwise an intense silence held.

"I am needed," Stal repeated smoothly. "Do you see, Michel? And you are needed too. In this way, good can come from even a very long life, if it is spent in the service of the proper cause; a life filled, in its own way, with satisfactions." A sort of ripple of expression passed over the man's eyes, giving Michel the impression that Stal had almost winked at him.

"Co-ordinator?" In the middle of the word, Michel's voice threatened to crack. "If this man wants to die, kill him right now. It'll make me happier to see him dead. It'll keep my mind more stable."

The man started a movement toward Michel, and like a broken robot stopped in the middle of it. The mask-like expression of his face had broken also, in an upwelling of fear, and for a few moments he had to struggle to maintain control.

"It is improbable, Michel," the Co-ordinator commented, "that you have ever ordered a human life-unit's termination before. Therefore I compute that your mental stability will not be served by such an action now. Therefore your order will not now be obeyed." And with that, the day's interview was at an end; and it was a long time before Michel saw Stal again.

Even before that incident, he had rarely encountered Elly and the goodlife in the same room. It had to be that the machine was, for whatever reasons, keeping them apart. Elly, like Michel, had some choice of movement about the ship, and like him she was always escorted by at least one robot. No sudden attempt by either of them to launch the ship's lifeboat, or disable a control system, was going to have the least chance of success.

By mutual unspoken agreement, Michel's conversations with Elly were always guarded, as it was certain that the Co-ordinator would always be listening by one means or another. Outside of their imprisonment, nothing grossly horrible was being done to either of them. But Elly, at least, no longer looked healthy. She had lost weight, so that the gray Temple clothes hung loosely on her body. When Michel mentioned this, she calmly agreed. But she did not seem to think it mattered much.

"How are *you* bearing up?" she asked him, reaching to cup a hand under his chin and tilt his face up to the light. At this gesture their respective guardian machines each leaned a few centimeters closer, presumably ready to block any attempt at strangling the Co-ordinator's prize specimen.

"Well enough," he answered readily. And he really was; he didn't know why or how, but it was so. "You know, I think I'm growing. This suit is starting to feel tight." The orange gym-suit, run through his cabin's laundry ducts at intervals, was still the only clothing that he had.

"Yes, I suppose you are." Elly sounded as if her own idea of time had grown as vague as his. She looked at him strangely. "But your hair is shorter than it was."

"The machines cut it." Reducing the length of each strand by what Michel had decided must have been a standard number of centimeters. "Elly, if you're really my mother—"

"Yes?"

"Who's my biofather, then?" He had decided

that the machines must already have got some answer from her to that question; he couldn't see how it was going to matter that they would overhear her repetition of the answer now.

But the Co-ordinator, speaking through one of its robots, immediately warned her: "Give no answer." Elly looked wearily away, kept silent.

Michel raised his eyes. "Why shouldn't I know?" he demanded of the low metallic overhead.

"The future only is alterable. What is past cannot be changed."

A few hours after that—or was it a few days, perhaps?—Michel was alone in his cabin when one of the robots brought him new clothing, evidently just fabricated aboard. It was a somewhat miniaturized Stal-outfit, even including metallic-looking boots. Casual dress on shipboard did not usually include footwear of any kind, and these . . . Michel considered refusing the whole package. But then another idea suggested itself.

He changed into the other new garments, a loose shirt and short trousers of bright gray. Then, carrying his old orange garb in one hand and the rejected new boots in the other, he walked out of his room without being stopped. With his metal attendant staying just a pace behind him, he paced the few meters of corridor and entered the control room.

"Here," he said as casually as possible. "I don't need these." And with a double toss he lobbed the boots at the foot of the Co-ordinator's console perch, and the orange suit right at the captain's chair. On that chair Lancelot still lay, unchanged, wave-complexes shimmering through the seamless fabric of entwined forces.

The boots thunked lightly on the deck, the suit came down right in the outstretched hand of the robot standing protectively beside the chair, the robot that had been behind Michel when the toss started.

He was learning a few facts here and a few there. The only attack he was ever going to be able to make on the Co-ordinator would be of a non-physical kind, through what passed for the Co-ordinator's mind.

We're human beings. We're the bosses when it comes to any kind of partnership with machines. And also we're gonna win the war. If anyone should ask you.

But first, Frank, I am going to have to learn enough.

"Do you wish to put on Lancelot again?" the Co-ordinator asked Michel suddenly.

"Will you let me, if I do?" And now, he thought, I predict that it will counter with yet another question of its own.

"Not yet. I am not authorized to do so. Perhaps the Directors will allow it. What did you think of, when you first wore Lancelot?"

It had asked him that at least once before, at a time that now seemed long, long ago. What had he answered then?

"I thought of a time when I was in a play." Having given this answer, Michel was asked to explain briefly what a play was. He did so, though he was not at all sure that his questioner did not already know.

"And what role in the play was yours?"

"I was Oberon."

"On a stage you played the role of the fifth major satellite of Uranus?"

"No, of a—creature. I guess the one the satellite was named for. A story-creature. Fiction. And in the play I wore these robes that looked something like Lancelot. Quite a coincidence."

"What is coincidence?" the berserker asked.

"You must know the answer to that one better than I do," he told it. "Why do you keep on asking me questions where you already know the answers?"

"As you know, I am concerned that your mind does not change a great deal while you are in my care. Therefore I test your responses. Repeat, what is coincidence?"

Therefore you are losing, he thought. I couldn't keep my mind from changing even if I wanted to. "I guess," he said, "coincidence is things happening at the same time without any good reason for it."

"Was the story-creature Lancelot in the same play as Oberon?"

"No, in another story. And Lancelot never wore robes like—"

"Here there will be no play."

"I never thought there—"

"In approximately fifty-five standard minutes this ship will dock at a facility where you will be thoroughly examined. Then within a few standard hours our voyage will resume, with a stronger escort, and aboard a different ship where you will have more room and be more comfortable."

A dozen tentative plans, more gossamer than Lancelot's outermost fringes, were dissolved to nothingness by a few words. He had not foreseen this. Maybe there was some excuse for the failure and maybe not, but he just had not foreseen this at all. Yet there was nothing illogical about it; berserkers must have their bases, just as did human fleets. And there was no reason why the first base their flight came to should be the one at which his ultimate interrogators were waiting.

All Michel said was: "Elly? What about her?"

"Do you wish that your mother continue the journey with you?"

It seemed obvious what was likely to happen to Elly if he said *no*; what was not so obvious was whether or not she would be ultimately better off that way. "Yes," said Michel at last. Then he asked the machine, "What is this facility like, where we are going to dock?"

"I will clear a screen and you can observe it as we approach."

If he had asked for a screen a standard day or a standard month ago, might it have cleared one for him then? But they had been in almost continuous c-plus travel anyway, and there would have been nothing to see but fireworks.

A few minutes later, making adjustments on one of the control room's large screens (while his guardian stood motionless exactly between him and the captain's chair), Michel discovered a darkly massive body at a distance of about two hundred thousand kilometers and closing rapidly. Too big to be any ordinary ship, the object radiated enough warmth to be plainly visible in the infrared, while remaining obscure even under magnification in the ordinarily visible wavelengths.

The goodlife ship, having slowed drastically from interstellar speeds, was approaching the thing now at about a thousand kilometers per second, and still decelerating strongly. The image of the berserker base waiting ahead was still largely obscured by dust and noise; and this, Michel was thinking to himself, must be what gave him the sense, in observing it, of something . . . not as it should be.

Something out of phase.

Something—wrong?

Of course any berserker construct had to be considered wrong, from a purely human point of view. But this one had about it something that was odd, even given its bad purpose. He couldn't put his finger on it, quite . . . maybe he was just being affected by his own rekindling fear. The Co-ordinator had been programmed to be good to him, but what if the computers at this base had lately received orders to the contrary?

At Michel's back, reassuring as usual, the Co-ordinator was now saying: "On the new ship, you and your mother will be able—"

The berserker thing on the screen was definitely not what it should be, and now abruptly the words broke off. Warned by something other than a conscious thought, Michel had just time to turn and crouch and take hold of a stanchion before full emergency normal-space acceleration ate upward through the artificial gravity to grab at him and pull him down and spread him on the deck. His guardian robot, immensely stronger, crouched above him, its four limbs forming a protective cage. The direction of acceleration shifted without warning. From the captain's chair, Lancelot like a suddenly living cape came flowing toward Michel. The brief silent waterfall of Lancelot's movement was intercepted by one of the robot's deft hands. The machine swirled folds of cape around its fist, neatly forestalling Michel's own nearly hopeless effort at lifting an arm in that direction.

Somewhere beyond the now-closed doors of the control room, a goodlife woman's voice was screaming. As his own mother had once screamed, beyond a door. . . .

He was going to black out in a minute, if the acceleration did not ease. Some god of space swung a great club against the ship's hull from outside. The overload of gravities moderated, shifted again. It vanished momentarily, then came back stronger than before. Now entangled with

the robot, which had abruptly gone stiff and awk-
ward in its posture, Michel slid several meters
across the deck, skinning his knees and coming to
a weighty stop right at the base of the Co-
ordinator's columnar perch. The arm with which
the robot had seized Lancelot was enveloped now
in a mass of churning Lancelot-folds, which were
flowing up around the machine's shoulders, like
liquid in a capillary tube.

When gravity eased again, Michel plunged both
of his hands into the fabric also. The sensation
was familiar and shocking at the same time; he
had started to forget what it was like to feel complete, or almost complete. Even this partial contact altered his senses and increased his strength.
His memory of events that had happened since
Lancelot was stripped from him took on an unreal
quality, as if they formed an unpleasant dream
from which he had now started to awake.

The Co-ordinator was silent, whether through
damage or simply because dealing with the external emergency was taking all its capacity. The robot was almost completely passive now, but still
it gripped Lancelot with one hand and arm and
Michel could not immediately peel it free. With a
great effort, moving between throbs of high gravity, he got himself out from under the collapsed
metal body. And with a greater effort still, drawing what power he could through the contact of
his hands with Lancelot, he surged momentarily
to his feet and aimed his falling body into the captain's padded chair. Once lodged there, with both
his hands still muffed in the material of Lancelot
as in a reversed sweater, Michel unfolded and
closed the chair's body and leg clasps, designed to
hold in the occupant against emergency acceleration overloads and other forces.

He secured himself barely in time. A new switch

in force vectors threw the robot up and against the chair and console with an impact that almost numbed his right shoulder even through the protective pads.

Michel had the chair, but the Co-ordinator still held the ship. And now at last it was talking to him again, both ends of its speech swallowed in a twinned road of combat noise with which the hull reverberated.

"—adlife will kill you, Mich—"

Maybe they would; but at any moment now the Co-ordinator itself would be trying to kill him too, rather than give the humans the faintest chance of getting him back alive. You have been tricked, Co-ordinator, and are about to be defeated—your side is not the only one that can take a base by surprise, or set an ambush.

Michel in the chair, the half-paralyzed robot on the deck, struggled for control of Lancelot.

There came a microjump—the Co-ordinator still had hopes of getting him away alive—an interval of weightless fall, a jump again, blending at the end into another smash of weaponry. Whoever was attacking had not yet been shaken off. The robot, with one whole arm and shoulder now buried in the creeping embrace of Lancelot, was flung completely across the room, smashing unhardened civilian instruments at the end of its trajectory. Had Lancelot been real cloth it would have been torn apart, or else Michel's arms would have been wrenched out of their sockets. As matters actually stood, the fields of Lancelot stretched easily. And now, with a swirling motion of both hands, Michel could loop the stretched material round the Co-ordinator's post. The billowing folds created by the swirl almost filled the whole confined space of the control room. Contact was made, and for a long horrible moment Michel/Lancelot could see directly into the innerness of the berserker brain, all power and skill and emptiness.

In rage and loathing, Michel sent through the fields the full impact of his will. At the far side of the room the robot jerked once, like an electrocuted fish, then lay completely still. The Coordinator itself was more heavily shielded, and more durable as well; what happened to it was more complex, but it too was at least temporarily disabled.

The ship lurched through a final microjump. Simultaneously the loudest blast yet shook it, like a small animal in some predator's jaws, an energy wavefront slamming the hull with such impact that the vibration rang deafeningly through the air inside.

With that, combat and flight seemed to have come to an end together. The ship was drifting, internal gravity failing fast. But at last the dead robot's grip on Lancelot was broken; when Michel tugged again, the force-fabric flowed resistlessly toward him between digits of inert material. Michel reeled the stuff in, looking for the fasteners, his fingers probing and sliding through the familiar smooth gauze, tracing out one nexus of quiescent force after another. At last a clasp materialized within his grasp. This was the one, he thought, that should go round his neck.

At Moonbase and on Miranda there had always been a squad of fitters ready to help him put on Lancelot and take it off. Here he had no help. But by now he had learned something, and had forgotten nothing, about how Lancelot ought to be worn.

When he had found the five essential fasteners and clasped them snugly to his arms and legs and neck, he undid the restraints of his chair and stood up. The room was full of electrical noise, and smoke, the monotonous throbbing of several alarms, the sound of a fire trying to get started. Michel moved at once for the control room door. It was jammed, but Lancelot wrenched it open.

"Elly—"

He called again, louder. Somewhere air was leaking out, a windy shine. In the near absence of gravity, an inert human form came drifting down a cross corridor, moving in the direction of the leak. Stal's booted feet dragged a little as if in reluctance to face the great nothingness that made the air itself scream so.

Not until Michel himself could get outside would he be able to tell just what had happened to the ship, and see what other craft might be nearby. But even before doing that, he had to see what had happened to—to Elly.

He found her in her small cabin, where she had been too late in trying to get herself strapped into a berth. There was blood in the air and on her clothing, and Michel thought from the limpness of her drifting frame that other damage must have been done as well. Probably some bones were broken. She was unconscious. Michel tried to shut the cabin door tightly again to save some air, but Lancelot had broken the latch in getting him in, and it would not close properly. He could feel a steady continuing drop in pressure. Near panic, Michel tore up handfuls of bedding and tried to stuff space at the edge of the door with it. Then he gave that up.

"Elly? Don't, don't die, Elly. I'm going to put you in the lifeboat."

She wouldn't answer. Her face was strange and still—how could he be sure she wasn't dead already? Somehow, choking himself though not for any want of air, stumbling, punching ferociously at any obstacle that threatened to impede their progress, he got her out of the cabin as carefully as he could, and down the corridor to where the lifeboat was berthed.

A minor booby-trap went off in his/Lancelot's face as soon as he started to open the boat's entry hatch; no damage done. Within a minute he had Elly inside, the hatch shut again behind them, air pressure building from the emergency supply to somewhere around Earth or Alpine normal. Gravity she was not going to need. Just as in the lifeboats of adventure stories, there was a medirobot here, and with fumbling fingers Michel attached its tentacles to Elly's arm and throat; it ought to be able to manage more connections for itself, as needed.

Half a dozen people could have managed to fit, rather uncomfortably, inside the lifeboat's passenger space. There was only a single berth. Before Michel had quite finished fastening her into this, Elly regained consciousness.

"Michel?" Her voice was weak, but it sounded almost happy.

Relief made him feel weak himself. "Elly, hang on. Don't bother trying to talk. Human ships are going to be here soon. You're going to be all right."

"You look so . . . you're my boy." Her voice was empty space, tinged with a little tenderness. Then it suddenly developed purpose. "Ought to tell you. Your father. Is Frank Marcus."

At the moment, the words seemed to convey no meaning. "Don't worry now," was all that Michel said, a couple of seconds later. "I'm going to launch us now. This boat should bring us out near our own ships. They should be searching—"

Just outside the boat, metal was yielding to a slow, grinding pressure. It made a scraping on the boat's small hull. Something was deforming the launch cradle underneath it, methodically, too methodically by far to be accidental.

Michel shot an arm toward the launch button, held it poised in air for four seconds of agonized, half-instinctive thought, then twisted the timer for a half-minute's delay, and hit the button.

Out of here, he thought next, commanding Lancelot. *But let no air escape.* There was a confused glimpse of the exit hatch hurtling toward his face, and then—

He was outside the boat, in the corridor of the dying goodlife ship. Behind him the lifeboat's hatch was still closed, or closed again. Around him/Lancelot the noises of tortured machinery rose and fell, and smoke stained the flying, failing air.

Beneath the lifeboat, a surviving robot crouched, exerting all its strength on the launch rails.

Lancelot flowed in movement. Some object that had been hard and strong convulsed in Lancelot's double grip, melting and crumpling at the same time, before it was flung aside. Then Michel/Lancelot bent to the rails, straightening them, restoring function. The launching, when it came, surprised Michel with a great flash of light. But it left him still safe, spinning in free space a hundred meters or so from the ship. He looked at once for the lifeboat, but it was nowhere to be sensed. There was only its vanishing zigzag track, which only Lancelot's inhuman senses could detect, a marked trail into layers of spacetime that until now Michel had been unable to perceive, running at right angles to ordinary distance. His momentary will to follow that trail was rebuffed. If c-plus travel would be possible for Lancelot at all, it would take time to learn.

Instead, Michel darted around the heavily damaged ship at a distance of a kilometer or so, reconnoitering nearby space. That the lifeboat had gone without him did not alarm him greatly; he was still expecting human ships to appear on the scene at any moment, and even if their arrival took considerable time he felt confident about his own survival as long as he was garbed in Lancelot.

Meanwhile, though, the more he looked about, the more he was convinced that this was not the same stellar neighborhood in which the ruined berserker-base lay and where the human ambush had been sprung. The relatively nearby stars were simply not the same. Yes, his memory assured him that several c-plus jumps had taken place during the fighting; but he had been assuming that under combat conditions none of those jumps could have been very long. . . .

For the first time, now, it occurred to Michel as a serious possibility that the human forces were not going to be able to follow and find him here. The Co-ordinator's last desperate attempt at evading them might have succeeded. There remained the possibility, also, that berserker reinforcement might arrive instead of, or before, the human force.

While he was pondering this, radio brought him the Co-ordinator's voice, sounding no different than before: "Michel. Michel, come back." It was so like a deliberate mechanical parody of Tupelov that Michel had to fight down a near-hysterical giggle.

"You have nowhere to go. Michel. Come aboard the ship again, and you and I can work together for survival. You really have no choice."

He drifted, scanning space and stars. There were bright nebulae nearby—nearby as interstellar ranges went.

"You have nowhere else to go, Michel. Our last

jump was a long one. No human search is going to find you now. And there are no worlds habitable by humans within a hundred parsecs of this point."

There was no way to tell from a berserker's voice whether or not it lied. But as he drifted closer to the wrecked ship he could detect another sort of change inside it. The drive was running, storing energy, charging some component of itself as if for catastrophic discharge. There was too much damage for it to be made to work normally, and the Co-ordinator must know full well there was too much. But this charging could be used to improvise a primitive but mighty bomb.

"Michel. Come."

Even Lancelot could not protect its wearer from such a blast, not at almost zero range. Michel, as if it were a random movement, made himself drift very slowly farther off.

"You are all alone, Michel, as no human being has ever been alone before." In the pauses between the berserker's utterances, Michel now could pick up a trapped mouse-squealing. Not, though, from a mouse; evidently one of the good-life women still breathed.

"Come back. All alone, Michel, except for me. Come back, and stay alive."

He drifted farther still. Would it unleash its blast now? No, it had computed that it must lure him closer first, then obliterate him and itself.

". . . come back, and I will be the servant from now on . . ."

The ship was too badly damaged to let it chase him, even slowly. He turned and moved deliberately away. Ahead, at a distance that his perception did not measure in kilometers but instead in terms of being reachable in a matter of hours, began the fringes of a galactic nebula that might, for all Michel knew, extend for a hundred parsecs. What Lance could still detect of the lifeboat's fading spoor seemed strongest in that direction.

He had to follow, before the fleet gave up the search and left him behind. Movement fed fear, and fear turned movement into flight.

Going home. Alpine.

Home lay somewhere in the galaxy, and there was nothing to stop his moving toward it now, for he was free. The Co-ordinator had been left far, far behind him now, and so had Tupelov, and so had the woman who had so softly and insidiously claimed to be Michel's mother. (Some idea there had been, hadn't there, of following a lifeboat? But that idea could no longer be remembered very clearly.)

Panic. Got to watch out for that. Michel realized that he had been in a state of panic recently. But recently he had managed to master that. Just closing his eyes had helped. Closing his eyes and resting, drifting, here in this peaceful, restful spot.

Keeping his eyes closed, he allowed his breathing (which had recently been quite violent) to slow to a complete stop. With Lancelot you didn't need to breathe at all. Cramps wracked his guts for a moment, but in another moment Lancelot had taken care of that as well.

It was Elly who was dying, not his mother. It was a berserker who had first told him that Elly was his mother, and therefore that must have been a lie. They were evil and they always lied . . . something had been said about Frank being his biofather. That was too much to think about just now.

His real mother would now be . . . at Moonbase, probably. But soon she would be leaving there and coming home, home to Michel's father and to Michel as well. And they were all going to meet there, at home. Where else should a family meet?

Even if his mother hadn't quite got back to Alpine yet, she must be on the way. And his father was of course already there; somebody had to look after the business. Business included woodcarving orders, piled up there for Michel to work at. As soon as he had hugged his father he would go to his room and while waiting for his mother maybe do some work. First, though, he would slide under the quilted cover of the great carven bed, and get some rest. His bed stood by a window, a cosy window whose sky was blanketed eternally by a great Blackwool comforter that could keep out the stars.

His body wasn't really tired now. Not with Lancelot's support. But still something in him yearned for sleep.

Keeping his eyes closed, Michel issued a silent order: Let me rest, Lance, but fly me home. He waited, but he could feel that nothing was going to happen. Lance did not really know which way to go, that was the problem.

Opening his eyes again, unwillingly, Michel forced himself to study his surroundings. The scene had changed since the last time he had taken a look around. Certainly the wrecked goodlife ship was no longer anywhere within range of his perception, and he had no idea in which direction it now lay. Dust clouds bulking like thunderheads, within a few billion kilometers, kept him from getting much of a look at anything beyond, while at the same time the rest of the sky blazed with more stars than he really found comfortable. It was hard to gaze into them, Lancelot or not. His eyelids kept drooping and he felt so tired. . . .

At last (and the search took him an uncomfortably long time) Michel found an open line of sight through which he could just distinguish a few degrees of curving spiral arm that he judged must be a thousand parsecs distant. That arm, Michel decided after he had looked at it for a while, embodied a great curve that was centered truly on the invisible Core. At least, the three-thousand-year-old light of those far stars brought into his/ Lancelot's eyes a description of how that arm had curved three thousand years ago. From that information it was obvious at least at what angle the plane of the galaxy lay—that would not have changed much in a mere three thousand years— and also in which direction was the Core.

Quite near the Core, he knew, lay Blackwool Nebula. Michel looked in that direction now, with eyes that stung, and presently he began to move. Impatiently he dodged the wisps and specks of matter that flickered past him, impeding his progress by preventing Lance from reaching anything like his best true speed. Home. Alpine. . . .

And almost before he had dared to begin to hope for it, he could see the dark mass of Blackwool outlined plainly before him. His home sun was still invisible, of course, inside, but Michel knew that it would be there, a single bright jewel in a black velvet pouch, and round it the fragile ring of Alpine's orbit. In another moment tears had blurred his/Lance's vision totally.

"Mother," he murmured, stretching out his arms. Lance needed no conscious orders now. The specks of matter in his pathway thinned; the last fringes of an obstructing nebula were being left behind, in an eye-blink of speed.

When Michel's vision cleared again, he beheld an altering universe. The stars before him were gradually clustering together, in a formation centered on the nebula he sought. At the same time their light was shifting into the blue. When he glanced back he saw that the remaining stars and nebulae were clustering there, this time redly. All around Michel and at right angles to his flight, a belt of blackly deserted sky was widening. And now his own body began to appear distorted. His fingers were fore-shortened when he stretched out a hand; his shoulders seemed to be set far below a slowly elongating neck.

He knew these were illusions, and he thought about them vaguely, and in time a vague sort of understanding came: ride a fast flyer through a rainstorm, and the drops must appear to come from almost nowhere but straight ahead. So with light quanta if your flyer approached the speed of light.

Other effects had to be involved as well, but they did not matter, he thought. The point was that he had to be approaching lightspeed. Still the dark nebula with its false halo of blue suns remained apparently as far away as ever. He could not detect growth in its size at all. He was still crawling across a lifetime of black utter emptiness.

He stretched his hands out, far ahead of him, toward his home where his mother would be waiting. The middle portions of his arms ceased to exist, disappeared into his equatorial belt of nothingness. His/Lancelot's hands were distorted into a tight, dark ring, almost lost in blue starlight, encircling Blackwool nebula.

It seemed to Michel that he could hear a sound, the whistle of a heavy log-hauler late at night. Some tame machine signaling its need for human help, stuck somewhere on a winding road that threaded Alpine's glacial deserts and deep forests.

Oh, Lance, I've got to close my eyes. You've got to—somehow—get me home. Where I can sleep.

Lance would take care of it. Somehow. And sleep of a kind did come at last.

TWELVE

"JUST LIKE OLD TIMES, EL. OR ALMOST."

Come to think of it, she had recently heard those same words, or some very like them, several times. The voice they came in was rather mechanical, but most definitely human and achingly familiar. And this time, at last, the meaning of the words and voice had penetrated.

It was, oh God, it was truly Frank.

This time Elly awoke in no civilian passenger's berth, nor was she bound. She was wearing a service spacesuit, and rested in a scoutship's right-side combat couch. And once her eyes had opened properly she found that she was looking at the interior of a scoutship. Here and there her gaze lightened on an item of unfamiliar gear, but the basic outlines and colors had hardly changed in the ten years . . . no, it had to be more than ten years now . . . in all the time since she had served.

"Oh, Frank. Frank?" Looking through the comfortably open hatch into the opposite cabin compartment she could see him there as usual, boxed for combat, his armored personal hardware no more and no less changed than that of the modified ship around them. The scoutship that, when he was in it, seemed always to Elly to have become little more than an extension of Frank's self.

Unless ... oh, God, this couldn't all be some kind of a berserker trick. Could it?

"Frank?" she called again, and tried to move. Though unbound, she was too weak, and too well secured by the neatly fitting couch, to get out of it quickly and easily. Also, the attempt made her body hurt in several places, and she now became aware of several medirobot tubes that were patched into her suit and presumably into her body as well. Giving up the attempt to rise immediately, she lay back in the couch, not minding the mild pain at all; it authenticated reality.

"El?" came the familiar voice from the other compartment. "I think you're really with me, this time. Welcome aboard."

She muttered something hopelessly inadequate.

"I pulled you out of a civvie lifeboat back there. Remember that?"

From the feel and the faint sounds of the scout around her she could tell that they were making good sublight time. "Not being pulled out, no."

"But getting into it? From that goodlife ship? The important thing I've got to know is, were there any other survivors? That could be vital."

"There was a boy. He helped me into the boat, I don't know if he got clear himself or not. He had—he was wearing Lancelot. If you know what Lancelot—"

"That's him. Michel. Where is he now?"

"I don't know, Frank. I don't know where *I* am."

But Frank was muttering to himself: "I wonder

if I can get a scrambled beam through . . ." At the controls he displayed even less physical movement than was required of a pilot in a body of whole flesh, but Elly knew the subtle signs that meant that he was working. The idea that all this could be some berserker deception was fading from her mind, rapidly and gratefully.

"Secretary Tupelov direct," Frank was ordering. "Urgent from Colonel Marcus"

"Tupelov?" she asked in wonder.

"He's out here with the task force. Stand by one, El, let me get this into the pipe." Frank began spouting detailed galactic co-ordinates, which in their very remoteness from any she had been expecting to hear were somehow all the more convincing. ". . . and I'm bringing her straight back to the Big K. Towing the lifeboat on a cable beam, about fifty klicks behind me, just in case the bad machines tried any funny business with it." He interrupted his transmission to turn part of his attention back to her. "What do you know for sure about what's happened to the kid?"

She went into more detail about her last minutes aboard the goodlife ship; Frank sent off a little more information.

"So there's a task force," Elly said, when he seemed to have completed his transmission.

"Yeah. Well. I don't know how much of the story you know. If you were on that ship when we hit it, you must have been on it at the proving grounds. Don't tell me you've turned goodlife, though; I'm not going to believe that."

"No. No, I was taken along by force." She stumbled through an attempted explanation of her abduction from the Temple.

"Okay, if you say so. Good enough for me."

Quite possibly, Elly realized, not good enough for some others. But even to be accused of being goodlife seemed like a very minor problem at the moment. "There were goodlife on the ship, of course. Three of them still alive, at my last count. I don't know what happened to them when you people hit us. You've been chasing us, all the way from Sol?"

"More than a standard year now. More trying to intercept than chasing, and we finally did it. Tupelov's gathered a regular bloody armada as we've come along. Every system we've put in at, people have been ready to contribute a ship or two.

"Then we found a berserker base near here—I guess the brass on several worlds have known about it for some time, at least that it was in this general region, but nobody could get up the nerve to hit it. Marvelous what a crisis can do sometimes. After we hit the base we left the hulk of it in place, with some fake devices to respond to signals. Parts of our force went home again after that, but the Sol System people stayed; we've been on ambush station for the better part of a standard month. And then you—the goodlife ship and escort—finally showed.

"Tupelov's good at his job, you've got to give him that. He even brought the kid's mother along, just in case we might be able to get Michel back without wasting him. I admit I never thought there was a chance of that."

"Frank. I'm his mother."

There was a silent pause. Then: "You're wandering, El. They've done things inside your head."

"No. Why do you suppose they kidnapped me? He represents my terminated pregnancy—it must be thirteen years now, or thereabouts. It has to be that long."

"Terminated pregnancy—I never knew you had

one. Lady, I still think the bad machines must have stuffed all that into your head."

Elly shook her head, which felt quite clear. "Of course Michel must have had an adoptive mother somewhere, too. It might be her that you've brought along with your task force. But I don't know her name."

"Name's Carmen Geulincx. But I *never* heard anything about her being adoptive. That doesn't prove she's not, of course." Frank's voice became slow and doubtful. "But . . ."

"She comes from Alpine, doesn't she?"

A few seconds passed, in which Frank's boxes gave no sign of being any more than inert machinery. Then his speakers commented, "I guess you had some time aboard that ship to talk to him."

"A lot. But I wouldn't have had, unless I were his mother. The beserkers knew it. And Tupelov knows it, too."

"Well, when I get you back to the Big K you can talk all this over with him. . . . Hey, wait. Alpine, almost thirteen years ago? That's when you and I put in there. That was just shortly after—"

Again the boxes apparently went dead, this time so abruptly that some main power switch might have been thrown on them. Elly waited. At last Frank asked, "A very early pregnancy?"

"Very early. That's right, Frank. Michel is your son."

"You were ready and willing to kill him. You ordered him to be killed. Didn't you?" Carmen's voice hadn't quite broken yet, but any moment now. Her face was transformed into a stage mask of rage and hate.

Tupelov was watching her warily from across the big cabin, almost a luxury stateroom, that made up part of flag quarters aboard the *Johann*

Karlsen. He was thinking that Carmen was certainly entitled to some kind of a blowup, after all she had been through. But at the same time he felt he had to correct the exaggeration.

"Not exactly, Carmen. That's not fair. I just ordered that his ship and its escort be stopped at all costs."

"Not exactly," she echoed in a weak shout, and with that her voice gave way. Suddenly Carmen was looking about her as if for something to throw at him. There was of course nothing worth the throwing, since furniture, decorations and objects in general on warships had to be secured in place against sudden shifts of gravity or acceleration.

As she turned away from him and back again he had to listen hard to understand the rest of what she said: "For a year you've been trying to kill my son, chasing after him to kill him, ever since they took him away. And even now when that woman reports he's still alive, you give more orders that we're going to chase him on all the way across the galaxy if necessary, to shoot . . ." She broke down momentarily.

"To shoot if necessary, I said. If there's no other way to keep the berserkers from having him. Carmen, he's been with them more than a year now. How do you know he wouldn't be better off dead?"

Carmen got herself together and stood up straight. There was something new in her eyes. "Tell that to his father. Tell that to Colonel Marcus. After a year in space I've come to know the Colonel, a little bit. He'll kill *you* if you tell him that."

"He cares nothing about kids, even his own."

"Is that what you think? You never talk to him."

"Well. Regardless. Let him get Michel out of the berserkers' hands, one way or another, and Lancelot too. Then he can kill me if he wants." Not, he thought to himself while speaking, that there was really going to be much likelihood of that.

Carmen was at least listening to him again, and now he added, with concrete patience, "I really do want Michel back alive. Of course. Dammit, why do you think I brought you along—just to keep my bed warm? It was because you might possibly be of use to him and to us, keeping him functional, if and when we ever do get him back alive. Now it looks as if there is a real chance we might. Why do you suppose I've got the whole task force spread out right now in search formation? And if the search fails here, you're right, we're going to go on looking for him across the whole damn galaxy if necessary. Until we find him or we die of old age, or the berserkers learn to use him and they win."

"Why do you do that? Why? Because you want your weapons system back."

"We're fighting a war." Then Tupelov thought to himself that there must have been something better for him to say than that.

THIRTEEN

I'M GOING EVEN FASTER THAN BEFORE.

That was his first clear thought, coming as soon as he had begun to be aware of himself again and of the world around him, and for a good long while it was his only thought. The next one, after some interminable time, was a question: Should he open his eyes, or not?

Michel was somewhat afraid of what he might see if he did so. But certain physical discomforts had arisen, and Lancelot for some reason was not coping with them perfectly. They came in the form of unpleasantly constricting sensations on each of his arms and legs, also circling his neck and the middle of his body. Still, they did not prevent his moving freely. Grimacing, eyes still closed, Michel turned and stretched in space, almost as though he lay under snug quilted covers upon a carven bed. But he knew that he was still in space, and he sensed something about his speed, something he was not anxious to confirm with eyesight.

The sense of speed was quite internalized. And a similar inward feeling assured him that his flight was straight, in the sense that it was proceeding along the most economical course that Lancelot could find, toward his goal. What their passage might look like in terms of an objective pathway drawn across the sky was of course quite another matter.

It was necessary that he open his eyes soon, but he was really afraid to do so. With lids more tightly closed than ever, he willed first that his flight should slow. And with the willing he felt, as he might have felt aboard a slowing starship, the delicate inward jolt that meant a c-plus jump was ending.

Brought fully awake only now, by that fine jolt, Michel blinked about him at the scenery of the galaxy. With no atmosphere around him to impede vision, he had perhaps half a million stars in view as clearly focused points; only a spoonful out of the galaxy, most of whose suns were as usual obscured behind masses of nebular material, light and dark. And with his first glance he felt sure that the nearer stars were not the same ones that had been closest to him during his last clear look at undistorted space, before his building speed had blurred the universe around him.

The dark nebula that he had seen so clearly as Blackwool, and had yearned toward so desperately, had now disappeared, as completely as a sunset cloud searched for in the sky of dawn.

The bodily discomforts that had helped to wake him nagged at him still. Trying to investigate, he was surprised to discover that he could no longer see his own body at all except in outline. Lancelot had changed markedly, or had been changed by the experience of flightspace. What had been gauzy, tenuous-looking fields were now grown opaque. The whole apparent structure of Lancelot had turned into something more like a sheath of vaguely glowing leather than fine draperies, though it still trailed behind Michel in a comet-like tail. The fabric was now molded much more closely around Michel's head and shoulders. His arms and torso and most of his legs were opaquely covered. And it was at the places where Lancelot was fastened to his body that the feelings of irritation had arisen.

He could see out through Lancelot, with Lancelot's eyes, as well as ever if not better. But under the new surface of the protective fields, he could no longer see the fasteners. Groping to adjust them, Michel made the additional discovery that his clothing no longer fit him; in fact the garments were now grossly too small. His unseen shirtsleeves no longer reached much past his invisible elbows, and he could only relieve the pressure round his middle by undoing the waistband of his trousers completely.

No reason for this strange shrinking of his garments suggested itself at the moment, and he made no real effort to understand. Even as he regained his physical comfort by adjusting his clothes and Lancelot's clasps, Michel's mind was drawn back to the seemingly more important problem of the disappearance of Blackwool. Only now did the possibility occur to him that he had simply been mistaken all along about the nebula, that in his fear and confusion the first dark blotch he saw had appeared to him as home.

The more he thought about this the more probable it seemed. Still there remained a chance that he was somewhere in the Alpine region of the Galaxy, and one of the dark puffs presently in view—

there was an enormous number of them, scattered in front of starfields and visible against bright emission and reflection nebulae—might be Blackwool after all. It was easy to understand how distance could make the appearance of galactic features change drastically. Apart from the fact that to see a thing at different distances meant seeing it at different times, there was a simple analogy with planetary features as modest as ordinary mountains. Get close enough, and local details could not only change the appearance of the whole, but even prevent awareness of it. He might be now among foothills of brightness or darkness that were hiding behind them the one dark nebula he sought—even as Blackwool, when you were in it or beside it, could hide from sight the Core itself.

He could see nothing of the Core right now. This hardly proved that Alpine was near, but still he was free to take it as a hopeful sign, and chose to do so. It still seemed to him that the Core lay somewhere ahead, in the direction he had been traveling while he slept.

That was the direction in which he wanted to proceed. And proceeding, if he was going to get anywhere at all, meant making another c-plus jump. It had already been demonstrated that such a thing was not beyond the capabilities of Lancelot; it only remained for Michel to establish full conscious control over the procedure.

For the first time since he had awakened, Michel deliberately drew in a breath. The air that Lancelot manufactured for the purpose was no doubt excellent, but still Michel's lungs felt strange as they expanded to the full. Somewhere the fabric of his loosened shirt gave way. Wanting to make as sure as he could of his orientation, Michel rotated himself slowly in space, coming back after a full circle to face in the same direction he had started from. He still could not see the great starclouds of the Core, but he was convinced that it lay there.

The power required for c-plus travel was more than Lancelot, or any starship's engines for that matter, could extract from any known kind of fuel. So Lance was going to have to duplicate the functions of the much larger masses of machinery that made up an ordinary starship's drive—to detect and lock onto and follow into flightspace the force currents of the galaxy itself, the inexhaustibly rich streams of power that pulsed endlessly through the modes of space wherein mild worlds and human beings could have no natural existence.

He understood, now, that he was only beginning to know Lancelot. But included in the knowledge already gained was a certain understanding of the ways in which the wordless questions he put to his partner should be framed. To do it properly it was necessary to relax and concentrate at the same time.

Now, focusing his attention inward, Michel found and once more entered a door that Lance held open for him, a door into the strange and almost timeless realm that until now Michel had known only during combat. Now he could see that the currents that he and Lancelot must ride flowed here too, somewhere just below the floor of normal space.

This time Michel's eyes remained open during the transition, this time he watched all the fireworks of the c-plus jump. Chaotic radiation, unknown in normal space, fell in a random rainstorm, omnidirectional. Lance held a bubble of normality in place about him, and somehow found a pathway that made sense. Distance became something other than it ought to be. The shadows of gravitic masses existing in normal space extended here, and had to be avoided.

The shadows made an ominously thickening pattern.

The fireworks show ended abruptly, some time before Michel was ready to will its termination. Lance had, for some reason, aborted the jump midway.

For just a moment, when stability returned, Michel was not sure that Lance had returned him to normal space at all. They were drifting almost motionless amid a cloud of some kind of crystallized solids, a cloud incredibly dense for interstellar matter. The folds and billows of it reached away to mind-stretching distances, lit in remote parts by interstellar fires. Through Lance's vision, Michel could see each nearby particle as a regular geometric shape, exceedingly hard and pure. Lance could sense the atomic and crystalline structure of the substance, but neither he nor Michel could give it a name. None of the particles was more than a thousandth of a millimeter wide, and the average distance between them seemed to be nowhere more than a few score meters at the most.

The substance reminded Michel of something . . . in time it came to him. A hard stone that his mother had sometimes worn, set in a gold ring on her finger.

Just how far the fields of diamond-dust extended, Lancelot could not see. Certainly, in most directions at least, to distances beyond the merely planetary.

To slip back into flightspace here, amid matter of such density, was clearly an impossibility even for Lance, who could pass amid gravitic shadows where the hull of even the smallest starship would be far too large. Michel set Lance to carrying him ahead at the best sublight speed that could be managed. Then, overcome again by sudden weariness, Michel slept again.

When he awoke his mind felt clearer, and he was reassured to find himself still rushing forward, still with the strong feeling that he was going in the direction that he must go. The blockading particles had thinned out somewhat. Shielding at least as good as that provided by most starships glowed in the shape of a blunt cone, protecting Michel's head and shoulders. The fields of the shielding flared now and then with the impact of a particle, when Lance decided it was more efficient to hit one them to try to dodge around it.

Again, in Michel's arms and legs and neck, a strange sensation had grown up—not tightness and irritation this time, but a new kind of oddness. Still unable to get a look at his own body, he tried to investigate the difficulty by touch. Running his right hand round his left wrist, he was disturbed by the discovery that he could no longer locate the clasp whereby he and Lancelot were joined. Forcefields and flesh seemed to have interpenetrated each other to such an extent that Michel could no longer distinguish which of his sensations originated in which substance.

Trying to fight down a rising anxiety, he rubbed at his neck and legs and arms. The strange new sensations were not intrinsically unpleasant, and it seemed likely that he would soon get used to them if they did not fade. They gave no sign of fading; and presently he realized that his body was not only joined to Lancelot, but altered in itself. He seemed to be built more thickly than he ought to be. And his clothing, which had been growing painfully tight before, was no longer to be found at all.

He clung to the idea that these peculiarities

were only a result of Lance's necessary protective measures, making his body look and feel strange. Changes must have been necessary, for them to travel faster than light. When he got home, all could be restored to what should be. Lance would take care of it all, change him back ... then Michel's parents would put their arms around him, and he would be able to leave to them any problems that might remain.

Getting home was the important thing. Then all would be well. And Michel would be able to sleep then. Real sleep, long sleep, in the great carven bed.

His sense of the passage of time was still distorted; maybe, he reflected, it was gone altogether now. Because when he again took a careful look at the scene around him, he found that it definitely changed. The diamonds were entirely gone. Clouds of stars, looking thick as smoke but not with the utter density that marked the Core, hung before him and behind him. The starclouds were apparently motionless. Was Lance learning to compensate for the visual distortion that came with approaching lightspeed? Ahead of him there was also a lot of dark matter, material that might or might not be part of Blackwool.

Against the black matter ahead—and perhaps it was this sight that had roused him, brought his full attention back to externals—a patch of light was visible. It must be an enormous object, greater than any conceivable sun, yet it was irregular in shape as well as in intensity. Its spectrum, strong in blue light and the shorter wavelengths, indicated that Lance was screening Michel's eyes from the full impact of its radiance.

Michel at once changed course, to head directly toward the thing. Pure cold wonder made him forget, for the moment, that he had ever had any other goal. Even at sublight speed, the white apparition grew steadily in angular diameter. With an abrupt change of perception, Michel realized that it was not a bright thing seen against a more distant dark background, but instead a glimpse of light penetrating darkness from far beyond the dark.

With his approach the brightness widened, and intensified seemingly without limit. As Michel flew through the last barriers of intervening dust, he realized, with surprising calm, two things: first, that his flight had probably never yet brought him within sight of Blackwool; second, that he had a real chance to find it, now.

Before him shone the Core.

There followed an immeasurable interval in which it seemed to Michel that he was climbing. The sensation of the climb made him think of swimming uphill. To get where he was going he had to work his arms and legs, and this he did tirelessly, a physical effort that thanks to Lance brought no exhaustion though it continued without pause for a long time.

His arms spread like great wings, he swam, or flew, the galactic forecurrents almost to their upper limit at Galactic north. The globular starclusters of the galactic fringe burned round him and below him here like great bluish lamps. From each of his fingers Lance reached out with a kilometer of quasimaterial webbing. From Michel's moving legs there trailed a tailfan enormously great and tenuous, more like flame now than gauze or leather.

He reached an altitude where even to maintain his position required from him an analog of energetic swimming effort. His climb had reached its zenith, and it had brought him what he wanted.

Spread out below him now was the only existing map of the whole galaxy: the map that was the thing itself.

In very general terms, the view was like that from a low flyer hovering at night above the central lights of some great and distorted city. The enormous thoroughfares of the spiral arms were apparently bent a bit more than they really ought to be, a consequence of the remoteness of their outward portions from Michel, who therefore saw them at different times in the agelong cycle of rotation. The fiery clouds of the Core, some ten thousand light years just below him, were unresolvable into individual stars, even with Lance's vision.

And a first impression, which Michel had been declined to accept at first, remained: the Core, like that berserker base some time ago, had something wrong with it. Something . . . no, he could not guess the nature of the wrongness yet.

While he thus contemplated the map that ought to guide him home, he kept tasting distracting things, new kinds of radiation, through the shielding of Lancelot across his back. Incoming were particles of kinds Michel had never sensed before, and things that were more and less than particles. Things never allowed to reach the inner worlds, the cloud-shielded roads and ways where all humanity had led its small existence until now. The starship had not yet been made, Michel felt sure, that could climb here to sample them.

The unknown tapped his shoulders, beckoning.

With a swimmer's motion he turned his back upon the great map with the troubled heart. The deep-space siblings of the galaxy looked as they always had. From where Michel swam on his back, real space stretched out, holding the red-shifted spirals and barred spirals and squiggles and oddities, scattered out to the last faint sparks at the limits of even Lancelot's vision.

The beckoning was clear, and clearly there was no way for him to answer it. He turned back to his search for home.

The old space stories had mapped the arms of home for him to some extent, as had stray bits of conversation with people who knew some astrogation, in that short period of his life when such people had been around him. Now Michel decided, taking his time to make the decision, which spiral arm of the great map below must be the right one for his search. Once he had chosen an arm, he scanned it near its root, with patience almost that of a machine.

Until at last—and how much time that "last" involved, his mind refused to speculate—at last he could discern in that chosen arm a single small black nebula, of such apparent size and shape that Lance and Michel agreed it might be reasonable to think of it as Blackwool. A dot of pepper, one of a thousand similar dots, on a white sheet.

It was no more than a few hundred light years in diameter at most, and he was seeing it in a configuration of many thousands of years ago. There was no way in which he could be sure, yet something about that single dot continued to feel right. As if Lance could have senses transcending space and even flightspace, could be developing capabilities Michel had yet to guess.

The arms of the galaxy were reaching up for him, and he was starting down again toward his home.

FOURTEEN

HE WAS AT BLACKWOOL, HE WAS SURE OF THAT. HE HAD even been inside the nebula for some unknown time, working his way toward its concealed heart. Toward his home.

Once he had known exactly what he was going to do when he got home. What things he would do, and in exactly what order he would do them— and now, just what had that plan been, again?

While a part of his mind worried at that question, Michel kept on working his/Lancelot's way toward the inner depths of Blackwool's darkness. He no longer had the slightest fear of getting lost, wherever Lance might take him. By now he thought he could determine, from samples of the matter and the flow taken inside any nebula, approximately how big it was and in what ways it might be moving, and also which way he could proceed to reach his goal. This nebula, he was sure now, had at its heart a great hollow space swept out by the solar wind of one lone sun.

Was the Bottleneck still open, through which titanic ships had once escorted him in frantic flight? Michel didn't know and didn't care. He didn't need the Bottleneck, and so made no attempt to find it in the ebon labyrinths. Smooth glide amid the molecules of gas, the particles of dust, then microjump when he could, and glide again when matter got too thick. Thinking about it now no more than walking, moving now much faster than any ship could have made this constricted passage, he descended to the center of Blackwool.

He expected a bright gleam ahead at any moment now, and presently it came. Then, somehow before Michel had managed to feel quite ready for it, the sun that had lighted his days of childhood was floating in velvet space before him, a lone jewel set in the almost-perfect dark. To one side of the sun moved a lightspeck of reflection that had to be Alpine.

He supposed that if he waited here just a little while, long enough to watch a segment of the planet's orbit, it ought to be easy for him to tell just what season of the year it was at home. Instead of delaying like that, though, he ought to be hurrying on . . .

. . . and at just about this point it came back to him, his plan for what to do first when he got home. First he would greet his parents, certainly. Then—and he was no longer sure why this had once seemed so desirable—he had meant to crawl into that little bed of his and go to sleep.

There was some doubt in his mind, now, as to whether he would even fit that bed. He *was* still tired, yes, in a way. But truthfully he wasn't sleepy any longer. He hadn't felt sleepy at all for a long time now.

With a little cold feeling somewhere inside him,

he realized that he could no longer remember exactly what his mother looked like. There, he had the picture almost clear again. . . .

When he got home, no doubt about it, the first thing that he would really have to do was change. Lance would have a real job to do. The way Michel was now just—wouldn't work at home. But with relief he reminded himself again that Lance was sure to be able to change him back. Changes, hormones, Tupelov . . . it was a long time since he had even thought of Tupelov.

Suddenly he didn't want to look at Alpine any longer. It took Michel a while to remember how to close his eyes, but when he had managed to do so, darkness brought him peace. What next? Go home, of course. Something was holding him back; he wasn't pushing on for Alpine nearly as fast as he might have.

His mother's face at last became clear in his mind's eye. And with that, he had no choice but to go on.

Lately, whenever he was bothered by some upsetting thought, Michel had taken to stroking his unseen chin with an invisible finger. And now on his chin he could feel what must be, well, some sort of a beard. Tupelov, hormones, change. . . .

Anyway, where else was there for him to go? The sun was much brighter before him now, Alpine much closer in its lonely orbit crossing the velvet sky. The trouble was . . . again he could tell that there was something wrong. So it had been with that berserker base. So with the Core itself. And so it now proved to be with this.

The upper atmosphere of Alpine was all wrong. It was nothing but a great single cloud, glowing on dayside, a lifeless sun-reflecting shell of steam and water vapor and fine dust. It was much hotter than it should have been. All the adventure stories agreed that any once Earth-like planet that suddenly looked like that had been . . .

If any confirmation was needed, he could see that the once strong network of defensive satellites had been entirely removed.

He thought, or tried to think, about his parents. His head seemed to be filled with dull confusion. Yes, he remembered now, his father had been going to join his mother in Sol System. His mother really hadn't been here at all.

Numbly Michel drifted round the world to nightside. He listened for radio voices, and after a lengthy interval of silence heard one. It was not human; it spoke only briefly, and only in coded mathematics. It had a lot in common with that horde of voices that had once pursued Michel across a broken landscape, when he had been a small boy filled with fear.

He was ahead of Alpine in its orbit, and now he let the bulk of the advancing planet pull him closer to the deathmask of its poisoned air. Had his father really left in time? Had his mother instead come back? He thought from the look of things that all life must be totally expunged by now. The radio message he had intercepted indicated that some machines must have been left behind by the destroying berserker fleet, to make quite sure that the last microorganism was quite dead. But no locator beams came probing toward him.

Michel used Lance's senses to probe beneath the slowly seething, overheated clouds. Down there he could find the outline of a flattened landscape, but no remaining seas. Nothing to indicate that the berserkers' job had not been completed.

"Michel."

Round the limb of the slain world a small artificial satellite had appeared, moving in low orbit. It was revolving in Michel's general direction, and from it had come the radio voice speaking his name. The voice was familiar and unchanged—not Tupelov's, the other one.

"Michel."

He made himself wait, motionless relative to the planet, to see if the satellite would change course.

Activating a comparatively feeble drive, the berserker device pulled itself out of free orbit and decelerated, coming finally to a stop within ten meters of Michel. Its diameter was about the same distance, and it was roughly spherical in shape. In the gloss of its surface metal he could see himself reflected, a long-tailed spaceborne figure of living flame, his glowing body almost featureless except for striations like those of muscle tissue.

"Michel, I am your friend."

"How do you know me?"

"Your present appearance has been predicted." It was the Co-ordinator's voice, Michel felt sure of that. The Co-ordinator somehow, against all odds, found and salvaged from the smashed goodlife ship, the Co-ordinator's memory installed in this new hardware. That memory, then, was still something on which the berserkers placed great value.

"Come aboard, Michel." Only now did he take notice of the surprising fact that the satellite really did have a hatch on its side, of a size to accommodate a human. A casual probe of the interior confirmed that there was a warm, cell-sized chamber within, even now being filled with breathable air.

"Come aboard," it repeated, "and we will talk. I will convey you to a place where you can get the help you need."

"I need—" His own voice, so long unused, startled him with its harsh roar. Controlling it consciously, he tried again: "I need no help."

"But come aboard and we will talk. I have information that you will want to hear."

"My father?" When Michel waved an arm at the cloud-surfaced world below, a reflected glow from the movement came and went across the faceless surface of the machine that faced him. "What happened to him?"

"Come aboard and we will talk."

"Sixtus Geulincx. Where is he?"

"Sixtus Geulinex is quite safe. He was taken from this world before it was purified of life. The Directors now have him in their care, against the time of your return."

"And my mother, what about her?"

"Come aboard, and we will help you search for her."

"Liar!" The radio echoes of the shout rebounded from the lifeless clouds below.

"I was left here to be a guide for you when you returned."

"You're lying." But it just might be true, or halfway true at least. The cell inside might not be meant for goodlife after all. What must have happened, Michel realized now, was that the Co-ordinator's somehow-rescued memory had been replicated and grafted into a hundred or a thousand berserker brains scattered across an unknown volume of space. Each such machine was effectively the Co-ordinator now, besides serving whatever other functions it might be programmed for. Should Michel, or news about Michel, ever turn up, each one would be ready to deal with the event as the Directors wished.

Michel demanded, "Where have you taken Sixtus Geulincx? And what of Carmen Geulincx, and Elly Temesvar, and Frank Marcus? Which of them are still alive, and where?"

"I know only that Sixtus Geulincx is still alive. And well cared for, as I have said. He is with the Directors, and they are somewhere near the Core. My programming does not allow me to be more specific at this time. Come aboard, and we will talk more."

The physical form in which the Co-ordinator now confronted Michel had been built for several purposes. For orbital movement, for limited communication, to house goodlife or desirable prisoners if need be, to observe a purified planet and seed it with additional destruction if required. It had not been built for real fighting. When Michel reached out an unhurried hand toward it now, it had time to compute what the gesture meant, and then to lash back at him with energies intended to be murderous. But Michel/Lance's right hand went straight in through its nominal armor, to the key parts that Michel had chosen. In Lance's fist he squeezed them to something less than matter. It was done before the destructor charges lining the satellite's memory could be made to discharge.

Lance sipped at the satellite's power supplies, like some odd new lifeform imbibing electronic blood, gaining new strength in the process. Then, after some study, Michel removed more parts, deftly and with great care. The Co-ordinator's memory banks were open to his scanning now.

He scanned them and learned what he could; and when he had done learning, he seized what remained of the satellite in one fist and hurled it down into the clouds, where a new fireball bloomed suddenly and disappeared. The radio voices of other berserkers began questioning space around him.

Michel Geulincx, drifting over the world that once had been his home, came slowly to believe what he had learned.

Despite all that had transformed him, he was Michel Geulincx. After he had hunted down the berserkers still remaining in the Alpine system, he meant to go on looking for his father.

FIFTEEN

THE *JOHANN KARLSEN* WAS A GREAT GRAYISH PEARL, set firmly now in a rich jeweler's mounting of pearl-gray loops and bands, with the lesser roundness of a disgorged but immovable scoutship frozen at its side. When Tupelov at last emerged from the flagship, alone, he could see the vast, curved cagework of the Taj soaring away from him in at least three spatial dimensions. If he let his perception and his fancy get away from him, now with only his suit's faceplate between him and the Taj, he could easily become subject to the impression that here more than three dimensions were definable, that he was standing in the middle of an Escher solid made real, that he might be able to walk or climb away from the ship on one of these highway-sized, apparently unsupported gray loops and re-emerge from their distant tangles in a direction opposite to that of his departure.

Two days ago, meaning to investigate the Taj,

he had ordered the flagship driven close to it. Instinct and what logic he could still muster both urged him that the search for Michel had to lead here ultimately if it led anywhere; and this portion of the inner Core was quite alive with decaying berserker radio signals of indeterminate age. Whether the two previous human expeditions sent to the Taj from Sol System had had any success, or had been able to get back to Earth, he still did not know. Investigation was definitely called for.

He had been able to make the order for investigation stick, though there had been some grumbling. Some of the crew were whispering that after this last effort it would be time enough and past time to call off his monomaniacal pursuit of one human child who had to be dead and lost long years ago. . . .

The flagship's captain had driven close to the Taj, not meaning to enter it. They were close to the Taj, and then without apparent transition of any kind they were inside it, the intercoms exploding with the crew's surprise, the instruments jumping with inexplicable readings and then settling back—in some cases, to steady readings that seemed to make no more sense.

The ship was caught immovably. Two standard days of trying to work it free, using the drive and short-range weapons, had been unsuccessful. Huge gray bands of unknown substance bound it rigidly. In the bottomless space containing the gray bands, an ocean of weatherless air existed, according to instrumental indications. At last a scoutship was launched, with Command Pilot Colonel Frank Marcus and re-drafted quasi-civilian Elly Temesvar aboard, ready to do their fanciest flying. This attempt aborted at once, with the scout immediately caught in its own newly-formed loop of resistless gray, not ten meters outside the launching hatch.

There was urgent conversation between scout and mother ship, on various communicator systems, all of which seemed to be working well enough, but working as if the air surrounding the ships, an Earth-surface standard atmosphere, were a reality.

After that, there had seemed to be nothing to do but try to get out of the ship on foot and look around—oh yes, external gravity, if the instruments could be trusted, was steady and one-directional. Its value matched that of Earth-surface normal to four decimal places.

Tupelov, maybe feeling a little suicidal, maybe just trying to be fair, nominated himself to be first out. In this he was unopposed, which caused him a disappointment so faint that he hardly recognized it himself. So as soon as he was suited up, out he went, half expecting an instantaneous gray band to materialize in a loop round his middle as soon as he had cleared the hatch. Well, at least he would be able to come to direct grips with the damned stuff.

Emerging from an auxiliary maintenance hatch, whose door was thicker than it was tall or wide, and which closed itself invisibly back into the thickness of the hull the instant Tupelov was completely out, the Secretary found to his considerable relief that no gray bands had snapped him up. And also that he seemed safe from space sickness; the gravity felt as normal as had been reported. His booted feet were standing on one of the gray bands wrapped around the ship, and *down* was precisely the direction perpendicular to the band's surface where he was standing on it.

Other bands and loops ran in every direction, the nearest a few hundred meters distant from him. Gray and largely featureless, they appeared to be rectangular in cross-section for the most part, though already he could notice that a few of them were round. Everything was bathed in a cheerful and seemingly sourceless light, isotropic enough to cast no very noticeable shadows anywhere. The band that Tupelov was standing on—his exit hatch had been chosen for the easy access to good footing that it appeared to offer—was about five meters wide, and when he cautiously approached the edge of it outboard from the ship, he could see that it was about a meter thick. Beyond its thickness a downward glance fell through what might as well have been an infinity of distance. The farthest bands visible in that direction were backed by what appeared to be a very light gray sky, continuous with the "sky" that Tupelov could also see to right and left and overhead.

"Sir, do you read me? Sir, this is the bridge, over."

He shouldn't have let a radio silence grow. "I read you, Bridge. So far I've experienced nothing to indicate that our readings on ship's instruments were faulty. I'm just standing here on this band, whatever it is. The substance feels just slightly yielding underfoot—about like a good floor. Gravity feels normal. Also my suit indicators confirm the presence of atmosphere. Colonel Marcus?"

"Sir?" The answer sounded faintly surprised.

"Why don't you and Temesvar climb out of that scout now. See if you can negotiate the band running down in my direction."

"Yes sir."

"Iyenari? Why don't you come out too? Maybe we can make some start at analyzing what these things are made of."

The Doctor acknowledged; he would be out as

soon as he could get suited up. Maybe there was no need for suits. Well, Tupelov wasn't about to take his own off yet. While he waited to be joined by other people, the Secretary went on talking, for an audience that he was sure must include the whole mystified crew of the Big K.

"Even in the farthest distance, the bands look perfectly clear. There's no consistent pattern to them that I can see, no beginning or end, no sign of what holds them in position.

"And there's no indication anywhere of precipitation, or fogging, or clouds, unless the apparent sky surrounding us is something of the kind. Air temperature where I'm standing reads just over eighteen degrees C. No wind perceptible—well, we're going to have a bunch to do, if we get into research here."

Pausing, he found himself breathing deeply. Even inside his suit it seemed he could detect a trace of ozone, a fresh post-thunderstorm, mountaintop, ionic concentration in the air.

Gray light bathed gray roadways, but somehow the effect was not nearly as dull as he might have imagined. There was rather a pearly richness, as of cleaned air after rain. And the air *was* clean, as far as his suit's elementary instruments could tell, and moderately humid.

Elly Temesvar in her suit, approaching at an upright walk along a roadway that, from Tupelov's point of view, made a wild descent toward him, demonstrated that gravity seemed to be everywhere at right angles to the surface where anyone stood. She crossed athletically from one band to another at an intersection, "down" shifting with her, and was the first person to reach the Secretary's side. Lombok's secret report, which Tupelov had just managed to hear before leaving Sol System, had not entirely cleared her of suspicion

of goodlife involvement. But Tupelov had accepted her story of forcible kidnapping, and nothing in the years of the long voyage since her rescue
had made him change his mind. After all, he had
grabbed one Michel-mother himself, and was not
surprised that the enemy should have confirmed
his intuition in the matter by trying to grab the
other one.

"Ms. Temesvar," he commented now, "you've
been here before. Or have you?"

"You mean is this the same Taj that I described
to you? Oh, I think there's no doubt of that, although I see what you mean. This doesn't really
match the way things looked to me the other
time."

"It doesn't at all match the picture of the place
that I had formed from listening to your descriptions."

"No, no." Chin lifted, she was squinting off into
the distance somewhere. "But there's a feeling—
oh, this is the same house, all right. But I'm not
in the same room of it this time, if you get what I
mean."

" 'In my Father's house are many mansions.' "

She turned a puzzled look toward him, but Tupelov looked away. Marcus was approaching, a
collection of boxes grappling its cautious way
along the edge of a narrow Taj-loop, like some segmented caterpillar. An energy rifle was slung on
one small pair of metallic arms. Well, why not?
Tupelov hadn't issued orders one way or the other
about sidearms, though the past two days had
given no indication that they would be needed
here.

"What about you, Colonel? Does this bring back
any memories?"

Marcus' answer indisputably came over his airspeakers as well as on radio. "No. Everything on

that first mission is still a blank for me. But you're both right, this has got to be the Taj, and it doesn't match the mental picture I had formed from hearing her accounts of it."

Elly was turning slowly, seeming to scan the environment with all her senses. She said, "That time we were being actively examined, I'm sure. There was a sense of—pressure, of several kinds. Of confrontation."

Tupelov was intrigued. "I've never heard you put it just that way before. Confrontation with what? Or who?"

She gave the impression of trying to find words. Marcus, arriving, had gone right to work on the Taj-loop near Tupelov's feet with a testing kit of some kind. Presently Elly added, "You'll all understand what I mean, when things turn that way again."

"You think they will."

"I get the feeling that we've just been set here on a back shelf. Things made comfortable for us— air, gravity. Then—activity will come. There's something we must wait for. What, I don't know."

"Your Final Savior, after all?" There had been plenty of time for discussion of the Temple.

"Thinking about it that way doesn't draw me any more."

Looking into the curve-bound distance, Tupelov thought that he could see, after all, some evidence of atmospheric phenomena. Around certain intersections of the curving bands dim, partial rainbow arcs were visible. A few other meeting points had somehow generated faint but perfectly complete halos of refraction. It looked almost reassuring—except that, between blue and green, the halos held bands of at least one color that Tupelov had never seen anywhere before.

Maybe, the wild thought came, that's what happens when the diameter of the full halo comes out to equal exactly one third of its circumference. . . .

Iyenari was just joining them, having come out by the same route as Tupelov. The scientist bent to take over the testing operation; Temesvar, who had been helping Marcus, straightened up, gesturing to Tupelov that she wanted a private conversation. When he had acquiesced and the scrambler channel was set up, she asked him, "After we get out of this, do we go home?"

"First, do you think we'll be able to get out of it? Second, what are the chances that I'll have a mutiny on my hands if we get free and then I don't agree to quit?"

She sighed. "I don't know about most of the crew—six years is a long time, of course. But you'll get no mutiny from me if you want to go on looking. And Frank is with us, of course."

Again his curiosity was touched. "Marcus I can understand. It's become a challenge for him; he can't admit he's beaten. But you . . ."

"I know. I gave away my son once. Then I met people who didn't know him, but worshipped him." Her eyes came back to Tupelov. "You yourself act in a way as if he were your god, do you realize that?"

"Huh." Some similar thought had occurred to him, at night sometimes.

"Then I met him myself . . ." Elly paused; her face altered. Then she raised an arm in a slow pointing gesture, as if long-lost Michel might be running toward them along a pearly loop. Marcus, having just turned to rejoin them, swiveled lenses. Tupelov made an adjustment for magnification on his faceplate.

At a distance of several kilometers—it was hard to judge very closely here—green fur showed brightly on one road-broad curve.

"I think those are trees." Elly was now back on the general communication channel.

"Trees." The one word from the Colonel showed disgust but not denial. Any environment so horribly wonderful as to negate all piloting skills might contain trees too, without adding anything to the mystery.

Tupelov's eyes, backtracking along the road on which the supposed trees grew, got about halfway to the place where he was standing before they ran into something else that brought them to a halt. He started to announce this new discovery, waited for someone else to spot it first, then finally felt compelled to speak:

"I think there are some people over that way, too. A group of them seem to be walking in our direction."

Iyenari promptly jumped to his feet, checking his suit's telltales. No doubt he thought they were all being subtly poisoned by hallucinogens.

"I have them in sight," said Marcus' airspeakers. "Definitely people. Maybe twenty of 'em, walking in a rather compact group. Not suited. Looks like they're dressed in shipboard casuals."

The bridge was calling Tupelov. "Sir, we've got a big scope on them. Earth-descended, no doubt about it. And we have a tentative computer match on at least two people as members of the *Gonfalon*'s crew." That was one of the expedition ships whose fate the people with the *Johann Karlsen* had never learned.

Whose idea it was that his people should advance to meet the onward-marching group halfway, Tupelov honestly couldn't remember afterwards. Maybe his own. At least he authorized more of his own crew to suit up and come out. And with the others he was walking away from the ship. The gray band flowed beneath their feet, the shifting of its effective gravity holding them always at the bottom of its curve.

From the bridge again: "Sir, they don't look exactly happy to see you. Or exactly healthy, either. They look, well, like refugees of some kind. . . ."

And again, a few moments later: "Sir, there's a machine of some kind in the middle of that group—"

In Tupelov's suit, in all their suits at the same time, there sounded a brisk alarm. It signaled that radio code of a certain ominous type was in the air.

"Back to the ship, quick!" Before he had finished giving the order he knew it was unnecessary; and he knew also that it was quite probably too late.

All force-currents led to the Taj, Michel had discovered. At least they did if the Taj was what you were looking for. Once that goal was chosen, there was no way to avoid finding it.

Nor was there any way to simply approach it for a cautious look. You located the Taj, you decided to get a better look, and from that moment it had you enmeshed in its gray loops, embedded in its own peculiar space. Maybe a decision to flee, instead of coming closer, would have been honored. But as matters stood—

On integrating the Co-ordinator's memory into his own, he had recognized in it a new view of something that he himself had seen long ago. It was something he had seen through Lance's eyes, the first time he had tried on Lancelot. Something that was then being clumsily and inadequately modeled, on one of the secret levels of Moonbase. He had seen, through Lance's eyes, a technician labeling that model with a name. So Earth had known a little about this, even then. Perhaps Tupelov had known, even as the berserkers knew, how the thing that humans called the Taj was connected with the origins of Michel Geulincx.

After the successful completion of his hunt in the vicinity of Alpine, he had flown straight inward from Blackwool toward the Core. Almost from the start this passage had been quite stormy, marked by heavy opposing currents. There were storms of radiation in his face. There were cloud-columns of matter in several forms, marching out fresh from the Core's creative furnaces, material moving on its way to sunbirth from the all but inexhaustible fountains known to exist at the roots of the galactic arms.

He went on in, shifting from flightspace to so-called normal space and back again. He crossed through areas where travel in normal space actually was faster. Around him there was increasing evidence of an organization growing ever more complex and dense. Still he had come only a few hundred light years from Blackwool, a distance far short of what should have been necessary to bring him to the very center of the Core, when the Taj appeared ahead of him. He had reached his goal long before he had expected to.

Seen from outside, the Taj reminded him of nothing so much as an enormous geodesic dome. Its size was hard to determine, but he knew it was immense, bigger than a star. And at once he knew that the great but subtle wrongness that he could feel pervading the whole Core was centered here.

So there was the Taj ahead of him, and then without a single frame of transition there was the Taj around him on all sides. He was still free to move within it, but there was no apparent way out of the cage of its great gray loops and bands. Not

a trace was visible of the geodesic structure that
he had seen from outside.

This was the center of infection of the wrongness of the Core.

Mild, thick, planet-surface air filled the whole
volume of space that now held Michel, extending
as far as Lancelot could sense—but the air was
not the wrongness; this space seemed to have been
built for air. In the air were radio messages, some
very old and decaying, intelligence in codes that
were not human or berserker either, the same
messages passing and repassing, endlessly traversing a finite but large and unbounded space.
These messages were not the wrongness, either.

And there was human speech, quite recent, in
the air. And a scrambled berserker code, saying
that fresh human prey had just become available.
Even this was not the wrongness in the Taj.

Michel took bearings. In a hurry, he turned and
flew. In the improbable atmosphere, a shock wave
grew before him like a wall of flame.

He saw and recognized the *Johann Karlsen*,
bound in its jeweler's setting like a pearl. Along
one of the bands that circled the great ship, machines and suited humans skirmished. There must
have been a sortie from the ship, and now the
party was cut off.

The enemy units were small in size, not much
larger than the people, and the power they radiated was almost negligible. Halting above the conflict, Michel picked up berserker devices with one
hand after the other, squeezing them dry, drain-
ing energy and information alike into Lance's reservoirs. Surviving units of the enemy, on the
outskirts of the conflict, fled.

Now there were only human radio voices
nearby.

". . . what it can be I don't know . . ."

". . . unknown life form . . ."

". . . into the ship, negotiate from there . . ."

These voices opened doors that had long been closed, doors to realms of memory never electronically ingested, memories of a time before there had been Lance. . . .

Another voice, a woman's, receding rapidly, already faint: ". . . oh God, they've got me, help me someone, don't let them . . ."

From hands and taloned flame he dropped the mangled metal of his enemies. The fragments fell toward infinity in all directions. *His mother's voice* . . . he spun into a meteoric passage of pursuit.

Ahead of him the berserker survivors bore their captive away in flight. He had no feeling for any outer boundary of the Taj, but there was certainly a center and their flight was in that direction. His pursuit gained. A handful of machines turned on him to fight a delaying action. He burst through their precisely calculated pattern, leaving spinning wreckage that had not delayed him very long.

He could feel that the center of the Taj was somewhere close at hand, and indeed he knew as much from the last berserker memories he had just swallowed. At an intersection of three great curving Taj-bands, a vaster machine than any he had yet fought against was waiting for him. It looked less like a ship than like a space-going robot, and it was in the act of sealing something away inside its metal gut. With the sealing, the woman's radio voice that had never ceased to cry for help was muffled at last into a silence that even Lance's hearing could not penetrate. The support machines that had been inflight were gathered round the great one now; they formed their ranks around it, but ranks that left a peaceful pathway for Michel's approach.

"You are Michel Geulincx," it said to him.

"And you are one of the Directors." He saw now that, like the Co-ordinator, the machine before him must be only one of a number essentially equal in capability, sharing essentially the same programming and memory. The other Directors must be outside the Taj, though probably in at least occasional communication with this one. There was no one machine upon which the berserker cause depended, any more than the survival of life now depended completely upon any one protoplasmic organism.

There was no need for the machine to answer his naming. It waited silently, for attack or for his questioning, perhaps. It was a tremendously armored braincase whose only purpose was the protection and support of the berserker computer gear that it contained. In a moment it might hurl its legions upon him—he could sense that more of them were gathering nearby, coming from more distant regions of the Taj.

His attack would come when he was ready. And there was only one question that he still wanted answered.

"Father," he said to it, and laughed. He knew that if he had heard that laugh from somewhere outside himself, he would have recognized it as mad and horrible.

"Who has computed me your father?"

"No one has told me the secret. I have drunk it in with the electronic blood of your machines." Michel spread his arms in a wide gesture, and in one of the support machines a sensor triggered and a weapon fired. Lance brushed the beam of it aside as Michel went on talking.

"Two people's bodies came together, on all the levels of space. Cells from their two bodies joined, and a new cell, a third cell, a new person—but not quite—came from the joining. Not quite a person, because that was here in the Taj, and you were watching, and you interfered.

"Instead of destroying the people, you took the chance to alter the new life that they were making. So it was no longer completely human. Maybe it was no longer really a life, with something of your death down in the middle of it, in the controlling atoms of its first cells . . . I don't know the human words for all the different kinds of energies that make a thing itself. You had a hand in the starting of that life, and then you—"

The Director interrupted: "You are superior to all other life, Michel."

"All life is evil to you, so does that mean I am more evil? No, I know what you mean—I am superior to all other goodlife. I was born out of an artificial womb, and your devices were somewhere in that, too, monitoring, changing me a little here and there. You designed me to be what you wanted from the start."

"You are unique."

"The Alpine goodlife must have helped you a lot. Did you save any of them when the end came there?"

"All of them were saved from life."

"Including Sixtus Geulincx?" It came out in a great, echoing shout.

"The need for his service was at an end. The death he wanted was his reward."

Michel uttered a spasmodic, prolonged sound. It was less human even then that previous mad cackle. Yet there was something of human laughter in it still. The vibration made his flame-shape dance cheerfully in the mirroring metal of the Director's formidable armor. It was the hysteria of a god, of a giant tickled beyond all endurance.

The Director was waiting silently again. The interior of it held something warm and still alive, but resisted Lance's most subtle probing attempts to find out more, even as Lance was now deflecting the probes that the Director sent toward him. Never before had Michel/Lance faced a single antagonist as powerful as this. Michel could not tell what was passing in its electronic thoughts.

When he had at last freed himself of that laugh-like sound, he addressed his enemy yet again. "Father? Do you understand what a machine-crime you have committed? I am no goodlife. I never will be. Do you know what a sin against your programming it was, to take a hand in my creation? What you must tell me now is *why* you did it."

"Perhaps you are not goodlife; I have said you are unique. But even the creation of life is allowed me, if that helps me to destroy all life eventually. You were created to answer a question: Is the Taj living, or is it not? The answer must lie at its center. If it lives it must be destroyed. If it does not live, there may be some way to use it against life."

The Taj was . . . beyond knowing. So Michel felt now, facing toward its center, which lay somewhere near. The berserker was right, whatever answers could be found about it would be found there. Michel could not feel that it was life, or non-life either. It was what it was. But still a steady wind of wrongness drifted outward from the direction of the center of the Taj.

To the Director Michel said, "I think I was brought here for a purpose. But not by you."

"I tried to bring you here when you were ready to be used. My machines and goodlife failed. But here you are. The severely odd things of the galaxy tend to arrive here. Things that do not fit the laws appear as if in court. For here the laws are made."

"And do you want to make the laws, machine?"

"I want to do only what I must do. Now you will try to destroy me." It was not an order, but a prophecy. "And you will try to save the female life-unit that I carry. Trying to do these things, you will follow me toward the center of the Taj."

"I will not help you."

"You will do what you must do. Through me the Directors that are outside the Taj will watch, and we will try to learn what we must know."

Lance reached for the Director's electronic nerves. It launched no counterattack, but parried. Michel's hands closed on elusive, slippery hardness, on energies that froze themselves away out of his reach. In the timeless mode of combat he advanced, and saw the Director retreating, dodging, matching his own best speed. A lesser machine was caught between them and vanished, disintegrated in a great blast that rolled and spun its fellows away among the motionless, eternal gray roadways.

The Director was retreating toward the center. Michel advanced.

From out of the center of the Taj, chaos howled at him like a wind, and progress against this wind became difficult and slow. Michel saw now the bones of dead life-forms, failed attempts to go where he was going. And there were the husks of dead, age-old machines, sent on the same task. The grayness of the Taj itself had grown upon them; they might have been here, and ancient, before there was an Earth.

And side by side with the wind of chaos, order and law and arrangement marched out like armies. They passed, vanishing endlessly down the galactic arms. Shapes still uncreated moved by him, flickers of potential being.

Ahead, the Director still led him on. Farther ahead, the curving arm of the Taj that they were following turned into a broad and desolate plain. And ahead again, it was a spiral climbing to a tower.

The altered shape of the Director still centimetered its way forward. Beyond it there lay the very center of the Taj. The Taj was at the center of the galaxy, and at the center of the Taj, Michel saw now, the entire galaxy was located.

The Director had been destroyed eons ago. And still, somehow, the crystal-steel form of the Director led him on. It was barely recognizable, but still it could speak to him, by what channels he no longer knew. "Life-unit. Tell me what you see ahead of us. Michel. Tell me."

But Michel could no longer bear to look ahead. Nor could he manage to turn his eyes in any other direction.

It started to question him again. "Is this—?" it began, and then fell silent.

"What?" Inside the awesome armor of his enemy, the life of his mother still survived.

"Life-unit Michel. Is this the God of humanity that lies before us? Never before have I been able to come this far."

Something was wrong, ahead. Something . . . and he saw the nature of the wrongness, now. It was only that the center of the Taj was— incomplete. "God must be something more than this," he said.

"I compute," said the Director, "an imperfection there. It is not finished. Either you or I must . . ." It came to a complete stop. Then its physical forward motion began again.

"Either you or I," said Michel. He moved forward, and was almost able to reach the Director now. He could still advance, but the advance was changing him. He was no longer what he had been. Everything had changed.

"I no longer compute properly," said the Director. "I no longer," it said. Again it came to a complete stop. And that was all.

Michel could reach inside it now with one hand, and carefully bring out the life it had been carrying. He shielded the woman completely in his closed hand as he brought her forth. His mother was frightened, terrified, still sane only because she could not see what lay outside the hand that held her safe. The center of the Taj was so small that Michel might have held it in his two human hands. And it was a room, spacious enough to make a place for a great company to gather. And it dwarfed all the rest of the galaxy outside. It deafened and it blinded, so that even Lancelot could not look at it at all. And when Michel/Lancelot looked carefully into its great inner calm, he saw that every galaxy in the universe had its own Taj identical to this one, and he saw that the Taj of every galaxy in the universe was unique, flowing with subtly different laws. No galaxy was alive, and every galaxy carried in its heart the seeds and secrets of all created life. And each had an infinite purpose to complete.

A door stood open, leading to the very center. Michel saw now that each Taj chose from the worlds of its galaxy a company of beings, no two from the same world-species. These it brought into itself, one by one, to forge one link in a great chain, to help lift the universe through its next purposive step.

Here were a company of intelligent beings gathered, diverse live cells chosen to differentiate, in a gathering still incomplete.

Michel turned for the last time, and without moving from where he was he reapproached the *Johann Karlsen*. Opening the metal shape harmlessly and gently, in a way that he now understood, he placed his mother inside it and withdrew his hands. The ship was whole. The bonds that had held it fixed in the Taj were of no purpose now, and they fell from it like dead leaves, like circlets of discarded skin.

In freedom, Michel turned back to the center. Voices called him, of beings who were perfectly free and whose bonds could never now be broken. Beside a Carmpan whose shape Michel could dimly recognize from old adventure tales, one seat along their table-rim was vacant.

Michel took another step, past the lifeless Director, and with that all life that had been born of Earth came home to the Taj-heart at last. Alone and of his own free will, Michel Geulincx moved forward to claim his place among the shining company.

An Afterword to Fred Saberhagen's
Berserker Man:
"Life and Death in Dreadful Conflict Strove"
by Sandra Miesel

IT STARTED WITH A GAME THAT GREW INTO A TOURNA-
ment and the players' names were Life and Death.

In 1963, Fred Saberhagen needed a fictional
antagonist that could be defeated by a simple
games' theory ploy. With the opening line of this
story, "The ship was a vast fortress containing no
life, set by its long-dead masters to destroy anything that lived," he made his first move towards
success in science fiction. "Fortress Ship"/"Without a Thought" introduced the berserkers and began one of sf's most popular series. Fifteen years
and two dozen installments later, play still goes
on. As the author himself puts it: "What was to
have been an ephemeral menace has turned into
something approaching a lifelong career."

Although Saberhagen invented his mechanized
killers independently, the notion itself is not
unique. Theodore Sturgeon's 1948 novella "There
is No Defense" predates his first effort; Norman

Spinrad's Star Trek script "The Doomsday Machine" postdates it. But Saberhagen has applied the idea with more imagination and thoroughness than anyone else. His murderous mechanisms are the recognized standard in the field.

Saberhagen takes the unusual approach of uniting his series around a common villain instead of a continuing hero. The unpredictable, ever-changing berserkers are ideal antagonists. Their resilience keeps the format flexible. This is no repetitious "template series" mass-produced from a single design. Connected sequences within the series such as Brother Assassin and the Johann Karlsen cycle reach their own convergent climaxes without affecting the divergent paths of the other stories. In effect, Saberhagen is providing an album of battlefield snapshots as the war against the berserkers rages across thousands of years of time and thousands of parsecs of space.

Flexibility aside, the great strength of this series is in the power of its symbols. The life-hating berserkers are the ideal image of Death for a technological culture. They speak to our fear of mad computers and killer machines with jaws that bite and claws that snatch. Whether they are the size of asteroids or insects, the berserkers are as vividly horrifying today as the skeletal Grim Reaper with his scythe and flapping rags was in the Middle Ages. Saberhagen's sf does in words what sixteenth century artist Hans Holbein's *Dance of Death* did in pictures. Saberhagen pays homage to this tradition by casting a robot assassin as Edgar Allan Poe's Red Death in his story "The Masque of the Red Shift."

But Saberhagen goes beyond the medieval concept of Death as a just, even merciful avenger. (The checker-playing berserker in "Without a Thought" is not directly equivalent to Death the chess player in Ingmar Bergman's film *The Seventh Seal*.) Saberhagen has made his devices as near to absolute Evil as material things can be. Therefore they are the perfect enemy which can—indeed *must*—be fought without thought of compromise. So treacherous, subtle, and perverse are the berserkers, they resemble demons in metal disguise. All their actions are negations. Like sin itself, their attributes have grown ever more malignant with the passing millenia. No mortal victory against them can be quite perfect or complete.

Originally, the berserkers' Faustian builders programmed them for some specific purpose in a long-forgotten war. Ages later, their mission has grown into a universal crusade to save all matter from the disease called life. Guided by the random decay of radioactive atoms, these agents of Chaos are bent on undoing the localized reversal of entropy within living organisms. Their goal is a sterile universe ruled by probability alone.

Death wars with Life across the whole evolutionary gradient. The berserkers strive to push the cosmos backward towards maximum disorder while living creatures struggle forward seeking higher levels of organization. Saberhagen's contending polarities Life/Death and Order/Chaos recall the ideas of Pierre Teilard de Chardin, a modern French philosopher-scientist who sees all creation growing towards an Omega Point of spiritualized perfection.

However, Saberhagen places these evolutionary insights within a more conventional metaphysical framework. His attitudes towards Good and Evil are solidly grounded in traditional Western values. He shows Evil as the twisted, empty shadow of Good and rejects the Oriental view that they are only complimentary opposites masking an essential unity. (These same principles govern his non-berserker work, especially his fantasy trilogy *The Broken Lands*, *The Black Mountains*, and *Changeling Earth*.)

First of all, the berserkers are rogue mechanisms, artifacts that kill instead of serve. But their capacity to repair, improve, and reproduce themselves also makes them ghastly parodies of their living prey. They mock true intelligence and all its works. Yet however many worlds they destroy or sentient beings they dissect, they never come to understand why "the most dangerous life-units of all sometimes acted in ways that seemed to contradict the known supremacy of the laws of physics and chance." Light pierces darkness; darkness cannot grasp light. The berserkers remain locked within the confines of their own logic, unable to discover why men laugh. ("Mr. Jester"), wonder ("The Face of the Deep"), create ("Patron of the Arts"), or love ("In the Temple of Mars").

The coming of the berserkers is the supreme crisis for all living things. Intelligent creatures, animals, and even plants have roles to play in the resistance. No species or individual, however peace-loving, can stand apart from the conflict. ("The Lifehater"/"The Peacemaker" shows nonviolence helping overcome a berserker.) But crossovers between the two sides tangle the battlelines. Berserkers incorporate human tissues in their cybernetic devices ("Starsong"); men depend upon computers. A killer robot achieves consciousness in response to a saint's love ("Brother Berserker"); depraved men worship the berserkers to wallow in hate ("In the Temple of Mars"). Saintly Karlsen ("Stone Place") and devilish Nogara ("The Masque of the Red Shift") are half-brothers; vice and virtue coexist within a single mind ("What T and I Did"). Yet for every treachery there is some corresponding fidelity. Goodness prevails when the odds against it are greatest.

Unexpected good fortune, which J. R. R. Tolkien terms *eucatastrophe*, is a happy example of the many ironies Saberhagen employs in his fiction. From the beast that outplays a berserker by rote in "Without a Thought" to the messianic child in *Berserker Man*, irony is a recurring element in the series. The philosophical context in which this device is used hones it to special keenness.

Saberhagen often presents noble characters like Karlsen in *Berserker*, Brother Jovann and Matt in *Brother Assassin* conquering through sheer excellence, and vicious ones defeating themselves ("The Smile"). But he has other observations to make about success and failure—the race is not always to the swift. Metallic monsters can be defeated by lifeforms as humble as squash ("Berserker's Prey"/"Pressure") and shrimp ("Smasher"). Human weaknesses like vanity ("Brother Berserker"), subjectivity ("The Game"), and forgetfulness ("Inhuman Error") confound mechanical perfection. Unpromising people surpass gifted ones in *Berserker's Planet*. These ironic reversals express the Biblical view that neither strength nor knowledge alone suffice when salvation is at risk.

Saberhagen's sharpest ironies cluster around the goodlife phenomenon. Here the berserkers' temporary success in producing human minions paves the way for lasting failure. In "Goodlife" a man bred and reared to be a berserker slave uses his janissary status to destroy his otherwise invulnerable master. But other berserkers have better luck convincing humans to serve them. Collaboration with the machines is rare at first and done for self-advantage ("What T and I Did"). But the most fanatical traitors begin worshipping

Death in grisly rituals that feature human sacrifice. Their sadistic ardor seems excessive even to a berserker who "allowed the torture to go on only because the infliction of pain was so satisfying to the humans who were its servitors." The cultists infiltrate humanity's ranks and actually gain control of an entire world in one instance (*Berserker's Planet*). The robot-imitators are so infatuated with extinction that they radiate the same emptiness as their idols; but these servants are in a sense worse than their masters because they have betrayed their own nature.

Despite all their advantages, the berserkers manage to undo the work of centuries with their own unliving hands. In *Berserker Man*, Michel Geulincx, the human they had predestined to be the ultimate example of goodlife, instead became "badlife" of the most dangerous sort. A berserker Director presides over Michel's conception, the result of a loveless encounter between two pilots under fire. His biofather Frank Marcus is a cyborg noted for his callousness, superhuman reflexes, and curious rapport with his mechanical foes. (Paradoxically, Frank has more faith in the ultimate victory of life than anyone else Michel meets.) Michel is born from an artificial womb while goodlife agents and spy devices hover about him like evil fairies. As a last bit of insurance, he is adopted by a goodlife father.

Nevertheless, against all expectation, the child grows up to be an angel rather than a devil, a knight rather than a brigand. He is no Antichrist but the longed-for Final Savior. The powers so carefully built into him by the berserkers equip him to destroy them. In the words of a medieval hymn, there are unpredictable factors at play in the game:

To the serpent thus opposing
Schemes yet deeper than his own;
Thence the remedy procuring
Whence the fatal wound had come.

Years of effort to deepen the stories' meaning
bear fruit at last in *Berserker Man*. Despite his
popularity, Saberhagen has not been content to
merely entertain with adventure yarns. He has
quietly expanded the significance of his work beyond the immediate question of survival. Elly's
glimpse of "order and disorder alternating"
within the Taj hints at a persistent theme in the
series—the purpose of Evil. To Saberhagen, what
is chaos close at hand may belong to some higher
state of order from the vantage point of eternity.
His universe is in no way absurd.

Berserker Man completes the process begun in
the prologue to *Berserker*: the discovery of a
meaning behind the horrors of the berserker war.
The predators are the unconscious spurs to mystical progress in their prey because their attacks
are the occasion of good deeds which would not
have otherwise occurred. In spiritual as in physical evolution, there is no growth without challenge. The severity of the crisis jars intelligent
beings out of their complacency, indifference, and
selfishness. It forces them to recognize and react
to the solidarity of all living things. During this
apocalyptic trial, every creature must choose between Good and Evil. As C. S. Lewis describes the
impact of war, "We see unmistakably the sort of
universe in which we have all along been living,
and must come to terms with it." The berserkers,
like Satan in the Book of Job, are an Adversary
whose blows improve the subjects they mean to
harm.

Saberhagen reflects the traditional Christian

theory of the *felix culpa*, the "happy fault that has merited us such a Redeemer." As the sin of Adam led to Christ, the sin of the berserker-builders leads to Michel. In a more diffuse sense, the raw aggressiveness that seems such a flaw in human nature rescues the cause of Life. The serene Elder Races are unable to define themselves properly. An alien ally remarks in *Berserker*: "The very readiness for violence that had sometimes so nearly destroyed you, proved to be the means of life's survival. To us, the Carmpan watchers, the withdrawn seers and touchers of minds, it appeared that you had carried the crushing weight of war through all your history knowing that it would at last be needed, that this hour would strike when nothing less awful would serve."

What is true of the species is likewise true of the individual. For example, consider High Admiral Hemphill, "the man with the cold dead eyes," whose very name suggests the gibbet and the hangman's rope. His rage to avenge his slaughtered family has made him as ruthless as any berserker. But "smashing the damned machines" is a lawful outlet for his ferocity and justifies his bitter existence. (His mania might have taken a different turn—Hemphill with his red and black battle ribbons corresponds to red and black clad Andreas, the high priest of Death in *Berserker's Planet*.) "God writes straight with crooked lines," says the proverb. If the force of goodness can find a positive use for such as Hemphill, how much more can it do with Michel?

Michel's adventures fit the universal heroic scenario of separation-initiation-return which mythologist Joseph Campbell calls the "monomyth." Michel is taken away from his place of origin, endures trials with the aid of wise helpers, is reconciled with his biofather, rescues his mother, destroys his berserker sire, and returns to assume his role as humanity's savior.

The circle *Berserker Man*'s plot traces out from the Taj, around the galaxy, and back again incloses a smaller circle beginning and ending with the planet Alpine. This structure gives Saberhagen the chance to multiply symbolic deeds and figures, as in the case of Michel's plural parents. Skillful pacing makes the lad's transformation into a victorious paladin believable by moving him along in gradual stages from familiar, homey surroundings on Alpine to the Solar system, and then out to the strange wide universe beyond.

But Michel is not simply Everyhero. He is specifically a Child-Hero. (His nearest kin in sf is Tomi Joya in *The Space Swimmers* by Gordon R. Dickson.) According to Carl Jung, the Child archetype represents an infinity of possibilities and the union of conflicting opposites. Michel, born the heir of man and machine, matured into the perfect cyborg, Michel reconciles and expands the potential inherent in each mode of existence.

Jung sees the Child as the best correction to an exclusive dependence on reason. Michel fulfills this task by refuting once and for all the berserkers' dreary creed: " 'All life thinks it is, but it is not. There are only particles, energy and space, and the laws of the machines.' " He concludes the philosophical argument begun in "The Peacemaker" by demonstrating that life is indeed a superior state beyond the berserkers' mechanical reckoning. For Michel is an absolutely unique composite being—a human person with a complete human nature intimately and inseparably joined to a machine nature in startling analogy to Christ, the Divine Person possessing both a Divine and a human nature. When Michel triumphantly enters the heart of the Taj—a privilege forbidden

the berserkers—he does so as mankind's delegate
to the Council of Life.

Most of the details of Jung's formula appear in
Berserker Man. Like other Child-Heroes, Michel is
begotten and born under extraordinary circumstances. He is conceived within the Taj, a realm
of paradox where nothing is what it seems. Here
the known laws of space, time, energy, and probability are repealed because "either/or" has become "both/and." Taj, the Persian word for
"building," suggests the Taj Mahal, the world's
loveliest tomb. But this Taj is a structure not built
by hands; it serves as a kind of cosmic womb nur-
turing "the seeds and secrets of all created life."

Child archetypes are routinely aborted, aban-
doned, exposed on mountains, set adrift at sea,
persecuted together with their mothers by cruel
father-figures. (Greek myth is particularly rich in
examples: Zeus, Dionysus, Hermes, Apollo, Per-
seus, and Herakles.) Michel, too, suffers all these
things although in his case the mountain is a
planet and the sea is space. Still, in hallowed traditional fashion the humble foundling overcomes
every peril. The weakest becomes the mightiest,
the least, the greatest.

Saberhagen's effective use of mythology is based
on a sound instinct for shaping fundamental
mythic patterns. He knows how to make Life and
Death, Good and Evil dance in stately age-old
measures. The berserker series illustrates the kind
of relentless simplicity and conviction he brings
to his work. As he explains: "This idea fit me,
worked well for me, almost became identified with
me precisely *because* it came out of the bottom of
my subconscious and through the top of my head."

Saberhagen has used specific models and pro-
totypes as well as general ones—Chaucer's
Knight's Tale for "The Temple of Mars" and the

Orpheus myth for "Starsong." He has often borrowed from history: Karlsen and Nogara are Don
John of Austria and Philip II of Spain while "Stone
Place" re-enacts the Battle of Lepanto, 1571. The
cast of "Brother Berserker" includes St. Francis
and the wolf of Gubbio, Galileo, and Pope Urban
VIII. These parallels are appropriate, ingenious,
but occasionally a trifle too tidy. *Berserker Man*
weaves multiple strands of association together
with more subtlety than ever before.

Michel bears a strong resemblance to St. Michael the Archangel, Prince of Light, commander
of heaven's host, defender of mankind against the
malice and snares of the Devil. Mont St. Michel
was his greatest shrine in the Middle Ages and he
is the special patron of the Jewish people. Although St. Michael does not belong to the highest
angelic choir—nor does Michel belong to the most
advanced sentient race—he is the best revered of
all the angels. He is the particular foe of Satan
just as Michel is of the berserkers. Both beings
withstand direct temptations from their Adversary. Even Michel's long fair hair and weapon
called Lance recall the traditional attributes of St.
Michael.

St. Michael is a uranian ("heavenly") power and
Michel trains on a Uranian satellite, one of a set
of moons that bear Shakespearean names. Michel
had played Oberon in a school production of *A
Midsummer Night's Dream* and it is from the moon
Oberon that the berserker raiders come. This attack is the midpoint crisis of the novel and speeds
Michel's transformation from sprite to angelic
warrior. It permanently removes him from the
level of commonplace reality. Afterwards, when
his weapon's gossamer wings have hardened into
body armor, he is ready for his destiny.

Faerie references and the weapon named Lancelot also link Michel to Sir Galahad, the youngest, purest, and strongest of King Arthur's knights. Sir Galahad was Sir Lancelot's bastard son by a lady named Elaine whom he mistook for Queen Guinivere under the influence of magic. Michel's biofather Frank behaves like Sir Lancelot and his two mothers, Elly and Carmen, resemble each other. Both these long-awaited heroes rise above their tainted origins to reach a supernatural goal others seek in vain. When Michel joins the chosen band within the Taj as the last link in the chain of evolutionary salvation, he is simultaneously Sir Galahad taking his place in the Siege Perilous and entering the castle of the Holy Grail. Images of autumn leaves and molted snakeskins at the novel's close signal mystical death and rebirth, the theme of the Grail legends. An earlier stage of existence has passed away, both for Michel and for the galaxy. New growth beyond imagining lies ahead.

The wonder-war is ended, the cosmic game played out, and Life now reigns as victor ever more.